**She had no idea how long they were entwined that way—it could have been moments, it could have been millennia.**

Chloe drove her hands over every inch of him she could reach, finally pushing her hand under the hem of his sweater. The skin of his torso was hot and hard and smooth beneath her fingertips, like silk-covered steel. She had forgotten how a man's body felt, so different from her own, and she took her time rediscovering. Hogan, too, went exploring. It had been so long since a man touched her that way, and she cried out.

He stilled his hand at her exclamation, looking at her with an unmistakable question in his eyes, as if waiting for her to make the next move. She told herself they should put a stop to things now. She even went so far as to say, "Hogan, we probably shouldn't..." But she was unable—or maybe just unwilling—to say the rest. Instead, she told him, "We probably shouldn't be doing this out here in the open."

He hesitated. "So then...you think we should do this inside?"

Chloe hesitated a moment, too. But only a moment. "Yes."

\* \* \*

*A Beauty for the Billionaire* is part of the Accidental Heirs series: First they find their fortunes, then they find love.

Dear Reader,

No one was more surprised than I to discover I like to cook. But a few years ago in an effort to prepare healthier meals (since I'm not getting any younger—ahem), I gave up processed foods in favor of whole. Now I make regular trips to Costco for enough fresh produce and spices to feed a pack of wild badgers. If you knew my family, you wouldn't question the comparison. Two pounds of garlic and a pint of cumin? That *might* be enough to get me through the week...

As a Southern girl, I naturally love Southern cooking best. But I love Latin, Mediterranean, Italian and Middle Eastern, too. What I haven't gotten into cooking yet is French. So of course when Chloe Merlin, personal chef, walked into my story, she cooked nothing but French food.

Write what you know? Yeah, like that ever happens to me.

Fortunately, Hogan Dempsey, blue-collar mechanic turned Park Avenue heir, prefers chicken potpie and taco meat loaf. He and Chloe might disagree about what should be on a menu—along with one or two other things—but they both end up learning a lot. Not just about food, but about themselves and each other. And about what really makes us who we are and where we belong in the world.

I hope you have fun reading about Chloe and Hogan. Visit www.elizabethbevarly.com to find links to Chloe's favorite recipes. I've shared two of my own for Hogan—chicken potpie and taco meat loaf, natch.

Happy reading! (And bon appétit!)

*Elizabeth*

# ELIZABETH BEVARLY

---

## A BEAUTY FOR THE BILLIONAIRE

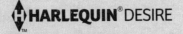

HARLEQUIN® DESIRE

Recycling programs
for this product may
not exist in your area.

ISBN-13: 978-0-373-83841-7

A Beauty for the Billionaire

Copyright © 2017 by Elizabeth Bevarly

**Printed in U.S.A.**

**Elizabeth Bevarly** is an award-winning, *New York Times* bestselling author of more than seventy books. Although she has made her home in exotic places like San Juan, Puerto Rico, and Haddonfield, New Jersey, she's now happily settled back in her native Kentucky. When she's not writing, she's binge watching British TV shows on Netflix or making soup out of whatever she finds in the freezer. Visit her at www.elizabethbevarly.com.

### Books by Elizabeth Bevarly

### Harlequin Desire

*Taming the Prince*
*Taming the Beastly M.D.*
*Married to His Business*
*The Billionaire Gets His Way*
*My Fair Billionaire*
*Caught in the Billionaire's Embrace*

### *Accidental Heirs*

*Only on His Terms*
*A CEO in Her Stocking*
*The Pregnancy Affair*
*A Beauty for the Billionaire*

Visit her Author Profile page at Harlequin.com, or elizabethbevarly.com, for more titles.

# Prologue

There was nothing Hogan Dempsey loved more than the metallic smell and clink-clank sounds of his father's garage. Well, okay, *his* garage, as of the old man's death three years ago, but he still thought of it as his father's garage and probably would even after he passed it on to someone else. Not that he was planning on that happening anytime soon, since he was only thirty-three and had no one to leave the place to—his mother had been gone even longer than his father, and there hadn't been a woman in his life he'd consider starting a family with since… ever. Dempsey's Parts & Service was just a great garage, that was all. The best one in Queens, for sure, and probably the whole state of New York. People brought their cars here to be worked on from as far away as Buffalo.

It was under one of those Buffalo cars he was working at the moment, a sleek, black '76 Trans Am—a gorgeous piece of American workmanship if ever there was one. If Hogan spent the rest of his life in his grease-stained coveralls, his hands and arms streaked with engine guts, lying under cars like this, he would die a happy man.

"Mr. Dempsey?" he heard from somewhere above the car.

It was a man's voice, but not one he recognized. He looked to his right and saw a pair of legs to go with it, the kind that were covered in pinstripes and ended in a pair of dress shoes that probably cost more than Hogan made in a month.

"That's me," he said as he continued to work.

"My name is Gus Fiver," the pinstripes said. "I'm an attorney with Tarrant, Fiver and Twigg. Is there someplace we could speak in private?"

Attorney? Hogan wondered. What did an attorney need with him? All of his affairs were in order, and he ran an honest shop. "We can talk here," he said. "Pull up a creeper."

To his surprise, Gus Fiver of Tarrant, Fiver and Twigg did just that. Most people wouldn't even know what a creeper was, but the guy toed the one nearest him—a skateboard-type bit of genius that mechanics used to get under a car chassis—and lay down on it, pinstripes and all. Then he wheeled himself under the car beside Hogan. From the neck up, he didn't look like the pinstripe type. He looked like a guy you'd grab a beer with on Astoria Boulevard after work. Blonder and better-looking than most, but he still had that working-class vibe about him that was impossible to hide completely.

And Hogan should know. He'd spent the better part of a year when he was a teenager trying to keep his blue collar under wraps, only to be reminded more than once that there was no way to escape his roots.

"Sweet ride," Fiver said. "Four hundred and fifty-five CUs. V-8 engine. The seventy-six Trans Am was the best pony car Pontiac ever made."

"Except for the sixty-four GTO," Hogan said.

"Yeah, okay, I'll give you that."

The two men observed a moment of silence for the holy land of Detroit, then Fiver said, "Mr. Dempsey, are you familiar with the name Philip Amherst?"

Hogan went back to work on the car. "It's Hogan. And nope. Should I be?"

"It's the name of your grandfather," Fiver said matter-of-factly.

Okay, obviously, Gus Fiver had the wrong Hogan Dempsey. He could barely remember any of his grandparents since cancer had been rampant on both sides of his family, but neither of his grandfathers had been named Philip Amherst. Fortunately for

Hogan, he didn't share his family's medical histories because he'd been adopted as a newborn, and—

His brain halted there. Like any adopted kid, he'd been curious about the two people whose combined DNA had created him. But Bobby and Carol Dempsey had been the best parents he could have asked for, and the thought of someone else in that role had always felt wrong. He'd just never had a desire to locate any blood relations, even after losing what family he had. There wasn't anyone else in the world who could ever be family to him like that.

He gazed at the attorney in silence. Philip Amherst must be one of his biological grandfathers. And if Gus Fiver was here looking for Hogan, it could only be because that grandfather wanted to find him. Hogan wasn't sure how he felt about that. He needed a minute to—

"I'm afraid he passed away recently," Fiver continued. "His wife, Irene, and his daughter, Susan, who was his only child and your biological mother, both preceded him in death. Susan never married or had any additional children, so he had no other direct heirs. After his daughter's death in a boating accident last year, he changed his will so that his entire estate would pass to you."

Not even a minute. Not even a minute for Hogan to consider a second family he might have come to know, because they were all gone, too. How else was Gus Fiver going to blindside him today?

He had his answer immediately. "Mr. Amherst's estate is quite large," Fiver said. "Normally, this is where I tell an inheritor to sit down, but under the circumstances, you might want to stand up?"

Fiver didn't have to ask him twice. Hogan's blood was surging like a geyser. With a single heave, he pushed himself out from under the car and began to pace. *Quite large.* That was what Fiver had called his grandfather's estate. But *quite large* was one of those phrases that could mean a lot of different things. *Quite large* could be a hundred thousand dollars. Or, holy crap, even a million dollars.

Fiver had risen, too, and was opening a briefcase to withdraw a handful of documents. "Your grandfather was a banker and financier who invested very wisely. He left the world with no debt and scores of assets. His main residence was here in New York on the Upper East Side, but he also owned homes in Santa Fe, Palm Beach and Paris."

Hogan was reeling. Although Fiver's words were making it into his brain, it was like they immediately got lost and went wandering off in different directions.

"Please tell me you mean Paris, Texas," he said.

Fiver grinned. "No. Paris, France. The *Trocadéro*, to be precise, in the sixteenth *arrondissement*."

"I don't know what that means." Hell, Hogan didn't know what any of this meant.

"It means your grandfather was a very rich man,

Mr. Dempsey. And now, by both bequest and blood-line, so are you."

Then he quoted an amount of money so big, it actually made Hogan take a step backward, as if doing that might somehow ward it off. No one could have that much money. Especially not someone like Hogan Dempsey.

Except that Hogan did have that much money. Over the course of the next thirty minutes, Gus Fiver made that clear. And as they were winding down what the attorney told him was only the first of a number of meetings they would have over the next few weeks, he said, "Mr. Dempsey, I'm sure you've heard stories about people who won the lottery, only to have their lives fall apart because they didn't know how to handle the responsibility that comes with having a lot of money. I'd advise you to take some time to think about all this before you make any major decisions and that you proceed slowly."

"I will," Hogan assured him. "Weird thing is I've already given a lot of thought to what I'd do if I ever won the lottery. Because I've been playing it religiously since I was in high school."

Fiver looked surprised. "You don't seem like the lottery type to me."

"I have my reasons."

"So what did you always say you'd buy if you won the lottery?"

"Three things, ever since I was eighteen." Hogan

held up his left hand, index finger extended. "Number one, a 1965 Shelby Daytona Cobra." His middle finger joined the first. "Number two, a house in Ocean City, New Jersey." He added his ring finger—damned significant, now that he thought about it—to the others. "And number three…" He smiled. "Number three, Anabel Carlisle. Of the Park Avenue Carlisles."

# One

"You're my new chef?"

Hogan eyed the young woman in his kitchen—his massive, white-enamel-and-blue-Italian-tile kitchen that would have taken up two full bays in his garage—with much suspicion. Chloe Merlin didn't look like she was big enough to use blunt-tip scissors, let alone wield a butcher knife. She couldn't be more than five-four in her plastic red clogs—Hogan knew this, because she stood nearly a foot shorter than him—and she was swallowed by her oversize white chef's jacket and the baggy pants splattered with red chili peppers.

It was her gigantic glasses, he decided. Black-rimmed and obviously a men's style, they overwhelmed her features, making her green eyes appear huge. Or maybe it was the way her white-blond hair was piled haphazardly on top of her head as if she'd just grabbed it in two fists and tied it there without even looking to see what she was doing. Or it could be the red lipstick. It was the only makeup she wore, as if she'd filched it from her mother's purse to experiment with. She just looked so…so damned…

Ah, hell. Adorable. She looked adorable. And Hogan hated even thinking that word in his head.

Chloe Merlin was supposed to be his secret weapon in the winning of Anabel Carlisle of the Park Avenue Carlisles. But seeing her now, he wondered if she could even help him win bingo night at the Queensboro Elks Lodge. She had one hand wrapped around the handle of a duffel bag and the other steadying what looked like a battered leather bedroll under her arm—except it was too skinny to be a bedroll. Sitting beside her on the kitchen island was a gigantic wooden box filled with plants of varying shapes and sizes that he was going to go out on a limb and guess were herbs or something. All of the items in question were completely out of proportion to the rest of her. She just seemed…off. As if she'd been dragged here from another dimension and was still trying to adjust to some new laws of physics.

"How old are you?" he asked before he could stop himself.

"Why do you want to know?" she shot back. "It's against the law for you to consider my age as a pre-requisite of employment. I could report you to the EEOC. Not the best way to start my first day of work."

He was about to tell her it could be her last day of work, too, if she was going to be like that, but she must have realized what he was thinking and intercepted.

"If you fire me now, after asking me a question like that, I could sue you. You wouldn't have a legal leg to stand on."

Wow. Big chip for such a little shoulder.

"I'm curious," he said. Which he realized was true. There was just something about her that made a person feel curious.

Her enormous glasses had slipped down on her nose, so she pushed them up again with the back of her hand. "I'm twenty-eight," she said. "Not that it's any of your business."

Chloe Merlin must be a hell of a cook. 'Cause there was no way she'd become the most sought-after personal chef on Park Avenue as a result of her charming personality. But to Hogan's new so-cial circle, she was its latest, and most exclusive, status symbol.

After he'd told Gus Fiver his reasons for wanting to "buy" Anabel that first day in his garage—man, had that been three weeks ago?—the attorney had given him some helpful information. Gus was acquainted with the Carlisles and knew Anabel was the current employer of one Chloe Merlin, personal chef to the rich and famous. In fact, she was such a great chef that, ever since her arrival on the New York scene five years ago, she'd been constantly hired away from one wealthy employer to another, always getting a substantial pay increase in the bargain. Poaching Chloe from whoever employed her was a favorite pastime of the Park Avenue crowd, Gus had said, and Anabel Carlisle was, as of five months prior, the most recent victor in the game. If Hogan was in the market for someone to cook for him—and hey, who wasn't?—then hiring Chloe away from Anabel would get the latter's attention and give him a legitimate reason to reenter her life.

Looking at the chef now, however, Hogan was beginning to wonder if maybe Park Avenue's real favorite pastime was yanking the chain of the new guy, and Gus Fiver was the current victor in that game. It had cost him a fortune to hire Chloe, and some of her conditions of employment were ridiculous. Not to mention she looked a little…quirky. Hogan hated quirky.

"If you want to eat tonight, you should show me my room," she told him in that same cool, shoulder-chip voice. "Your kitchen will be adequate for my needs, but I need to get to work. *Croque monsieur* won't make itself, you know."

*Croque monsieur*, Hogan repeated to himself. Though not with the flawless French accent she'd used. What the hell was *croque monsieur*? Was he going to be paying her a boatload of money to cook him things he didn't even like? Because he'd be fine with a ham and cheese sandwich.

Then the other part of her statement registered. The kitchen was *adequate*? Was she serious? She could feed Liechtenstein in this kitchen. Hell, Liechtenstein could eat off the floor of this kitchen. She could bake Liechtenstein a soufflé the size of Switzerland in one oven while she broiled them an entire swordfish in the other. Hogan had barely been able to find her in here after Mrs. Hennessey, his inherited housekeeper, told him his new chef was waiting for him.

Adequate. Right.

"Your room is, uh… It's, um…"

He halted. His grandfather's Lenox Hill town house was big enough to qualify for statehood, and he'd just moved himself into it yesterday. He barely knew where his own room was. Mrs. Hennessey went home at the end of the workday, but she'd assured him there were "suitable quarters" for an employee here. She'd even shown him the room, and he'd thought it was pretty damned suitable. But he couldn't remember now if it was on the fourth floor or the fifth. Depended on whether his room was on the third floor or the fourth.

"Your room is upstairs," he finally said, sidestepping the problem for a few minutes. He'd recognize the floor when he got there. Probably. "Follow me."

Surprisingly, she did without hesitation, leaving behind her leather bedroll-looking thing and her gigantic box of plants—that last probably to arrange later under the trio of huge windows on the far side of the room. They strode out of the second-floor kitchen and into a gallery overflowing with photos and paintings of people Hogan figured must be blood relations. Beyond the gallery was the formal dining room, which he had yet to enter.

He led Chloe up a wide, semicircular staircase that landed on each floor—there was an elevator in the house, too, but the stairs were less trouble—until they reached the third level, then the fourth, where he was pretty sure his room was. Yep. Fourth floor was his. He recognized the massive, mahogany-paneled den. Then up another flight to the fifth, and top, floor, which housed a wide sitting area flanked by two more bedrooms that each had connecting bathrooms bigger than the living room of his old apartment over the garage.

Like he said, pretty damned suitable.

"This is your room," he told Chloe. He gestured toward the one on the right after remembering that was the one Mrs. Hennessey had shown him, telling him it was the bigger of the two and had a fireplace.

He made his way in that direction, opened the

door and entered far enough to give Chloe access. The room was decorated in dark blue and gold, with cherry furniture, some innocuous oil landscapes and few personal touches. Hogan supposed it was meant to be a gender-neutral guest room, but it weighed solidly on the masculine side in his opinion. Even so, it somehow suited Chloe Merlin. Small, adorable and quirky she might be, with clothes and glasses that consumed her, but there was still something about her that was sturdy, efficient and impersonal.

"There's a bath en suite?" she asked from outside the door.

"If that means an adjoining bathroom, then yes," Hogan said. He pointed at a door on the wall nearest him. "It's through there." *I think*, he added to himself. That might have actually been a closet.

"And the door locks with a dead bolt?" she added.

He guessed women had to be careful about these things, but it would have been nice if she hadn't asked the question in the same tone of voice she might have used to accuse someone of a felony.

"Yes," he said. "The locksmith just left, and the only key is in the top dresser drawer. You can bolt it from the inside. Just like you said you would need in your contract."

Once that was settled, she walked into the room, barely noticing it, lifted her duffel onto the bed and began to unzip it. Without looking at Hogan, she said, "The room is acceptable. I'll unpack and report to the kitchen to inventory, then I'll shop this afternoon. Dinner tonight will be at seven thirty. Dinner every night will be at seven thirty. Breakfast will be at seven. If you'll be home for lunch, I can prepare a light midday meal, as well, and leave it in the refrigerator for you, but I generally spend late morning and early afternoon planning menus and buying groceries. I shop every day to ensure I have the freshest ingredients I can find, all organic farm-to-table. I have Sundays and Mondays off unless you need me for a special occasion, in which case I'll be paid double-time for those days and—"

"And have an additional day off the following week," he finished for her. "I know. I read and signed your contract, remember? You have Christmas Eve, Christmas Day and Thanksgiving off, with full pay, no exceptions," he quoted from it. "Along with three weeks in August, also with full pay."

"If I'm still here then," she said. "That's ten months away, after all." She said it without a trace of smugness, too, to her credit. Obviously Chloe Merlin knew about the Park Avenue chef-poaching game.

"Oh, you'll still be here," he told her. Because, by August, if Hogan played his cards right—and he was great at cards—Anabel would be living here with him, and his wedding present to her would be a lifetime contract for her favorite chef, Chloe Merlin.

Chloe, however, didn't look convinced.

Didn't matter. Hogan was convinced. He didn't

care how many demands Chloe made—from the separate kitchen account into which he would deposit a specific amount of money each week and for which she alone would have a card, to her having complete dominion over the menus, thanks to his having no dietary restrictions. He was paying her a lot of money to cook whatever she wanted five days a week and letting her live rent-free in one of New York's toniest neighborhoods. In exchange, he'd created a situation where Anabel Carlisle had no choice but to pay attention to him. Actually not a bad trade, since, if history repeated—and there was no reason to think it wouldn't—once he had Anabel's attention, they'd be an item in no time. Besides, he didn't know what else he would do with all the money his grandfather had left him. It was enough to, well, feed Liechtenstein.

Hogan just hoped he liked…what had she called it? *Croque monsieur.* Whatever the hell that was.

Chloe Merlin studied her new employer in silence, wishing that, for once, she hadn't been driven by her desire to make money. Hogan Dempsey was nothing like the people who normally employed her. They were all pleasant enough, but they were generally frivolous and shallow and easy to dismiss, something that made it possible for her to focus solely on the only thing that mattered—cooking. Even having just met him, she found Hogan Dempsey earthy and astute, and something told her he would never stand for being dismissed.

As if she could dismiss him. She'd never met anyone with a more commanding presence. Although he had to be standing at least five feet away from her, she felt as if he were right on top of her, breathing down her chef's whites, leaving her skin hot to the touch. He was easily a foot taller than she was in her Super Birkis, and his shoulders had fairly filled the doorway when he entered the room. His hair was the color of good semolina, and his eyes were as dark as coffee beans. Chloe had always had a major thing for brown-eyed blonds, and this man could have been their king. Add that he was dressed in well-worn jeans, battered work boots and an oatmeal-colored sweater that had definitely seen better days—a far cry from the fresh-from-the-couturier cookie-cutter togs of other society denizens—and he was just way too gorgeous for his own good. Or hers.

She lifted her hand to the top button of her jacket and twisted it, a gesture that served to remind her of things she normally didn't need reminding of. But it did no good. Hogan was still commanding. Still earthy. Still gorgeous. Her glasses had begun to droop again, so she pushed them up with the back of her hand. It was a nervous gesture she'd had since childhood, but it was worse these days. And not just because her big black frames were a size larger than they should be.

"So…how's Anabel doing?" he asked.

Of all the questions she might have expected, that one wasn't even in the top ten. Although he didn't strike her as a foodie, and although he'd already filled out a questionnaire she prepared for her employers about his culinary expectations and customs, she would have thought he would want to talk more about her position here. She'd already gathered from Anabel that her former employer and her new employer shared some kind of history—Anabel had tried to talk Chloe out of taking this position, citing Hogan's past behavior as evidence of his unsophisticated palate. But Chloe neither cared nor was curious about what that history might be. She only wanted to cook. Cooking was what she did. Cooking was what she was. Cooking was all that mattered on any given day. On every given day. Chloe didn't do well if she couldn't keep every last scrap of her attention on cooking.

"Anabel is fine," she said.

"I mean since her divorce," Hogan clarified. "I understand you came to work for her about the same time her husband left her for one of her best friends."

"That was none of my business," Chloe told him. "It's none of yours, either. I don't engage in gossip, Mr. Dempsey."

"Hogan," he immediately corrected her. "And I'm not asking you to gossip. I just…"

He lifted one shoulder and let it drop in a way that

was kind of endearing, then expelled his breath in a way that was almost poignant. Damn him. Chloe didn't have time for endearing and poignant. Especially when it was coming from the king of the brown-eyed blonds.

"I just want to know she's doing okay," he said. "She and I used to be…friends. A long time ago. I haven't seen her in a while. Divorce can be tough on a person. I just want to know she's doing okay," he repeated.

Oh, God. He was pining for her. It was the way he'd said the word *friends.* Pining for Anabel Carlisle, a woman who was a nice enough human being, and a decent enough employer, but who was about as deep as an onion skin.

"I suppose she's doing well enough in light of her…change of circumstances," Chloe said.

More to put Hogan out of his misery than anything else. Chloe actually didn't know Anabel that well, in spite of having been in her employ for nearly six months, which was longer than she'd worked for anyone else. Now that she thought about it, though, Anabel was doing better than *well enough.* Chloe had never seen anyone happier to be divorced.

"Really?" Hogan asked with all the hopeful earnestness of a seventh-grader. *Gah. Stop being so charming!*

"Really," she said.

"Is she seeing anyone?"

Next he would be asking her to pass Anabel a note during study hall. "I don't know," she said. But because she was certain he would ask anyway, she added, "I never cooked for anyone but her at her home."

That seemed to hearten him. Yay.

"Now if you'll excuse me…" She started to call him *Mr. Dempsey* again, remembered he'd told her to call him *Hogan*, so decided to call him nothing at all. Strange, since she'd never had trouble before addressing her employers by their first names, even if she didn't prefer to. "I have a strict schedule I adhere to, and I need to get to work."

She needed to get to work. Not wanted. Needed. Big difference. As much as Chloe liked to cook, and as much as she wanted to cook, she needed it even more. She hoped she conveyed that to Hogan Dempsey without putting too fine a point on it.

"Okay," he said with clear reluctance. He probably wanted to pump her for more information about Anabel, but unless his questions were along the lines of how much Anabel liked Chloe's pistachio *financiers*, she'd given him all she planned to give.

And, wow, she really wished she'd thought of another way to put that than *He probably wanted to pump her*.

"If you need anything else," he said, "or have any questions or anything, I'll be in my, uh…"

For the first time, he appeared to be unsure of

himself. For just the merest of moments, he actually seemed kind of lost. And damned if Chloe didn't have to stop herself from taking a step forward to physically reach out to him. She knew how it felt to be lost. She hated the thought of anyone feeling that way. But knowing it was Hogan Dempsey who did somehow seemed even worse.

Oh, this was not good.

"House," he finally finished. "I'll be in my house."

She nodded, not trusting herself to say anything. Or do anything, for that matter. Not until he was gone, and she could reboot herself back into the cooking machine she was. The cooking machine she had to be. The one driven only by her senses of taste and smell. Because the ones that dealt with hearing and seeing and, worst of all, feeling—were simply not allowed.

A ham and cheese sandwich.

Hogan had suspected the dinner Chloe set in front of him before disappearing back into the kitchen without a word was a sandwich, because he was pretty sure there were two slices of bread under the crusty stuff on top that was probably more cheese. But his first bite had cinched it. She'd made him a ham and cheese sandwich. No, maybe the ham wasn't the Oscar Mayer he'd always bought before he became filthy, stinking rich, and the cheese wasn't the kind that came in plastic-wrapped individual slices, but *croque monsieur* was obviously French for *ham and cheese sandwich*.

Still, it was a damned good ham and cheese sandwich.

For side dishes, there was something that was kind of like French fries—but not really—and something else that was kind of like coleslaw—but not really. Even so, both were also damned good. Actually, they were better than damned good. The dinner Chloe made him was easily the best not-really ham and cheese sandwich, not-really French fries and not-really coleslaw he'd ever eaten. Ah, hell. They were better than all those spot-on things, too. Maybe hiring her would pay off in more ways than just winning back the love of his life. Or, at least, the love of his teens.

Chloe had paired his dinner with a beer that was also surprisingly good, even though he was pretty sure it hadn't been brewed in Milwaukee. He would have thought her expertise in that area would be more in wine—and it probably was—but it was good to know she had a well-rounded concept of what constituted dinner. Then again, for what he was paying her, he wouldn't be surprised if she had a well-rounded concept of astrophysics and existentialism, too. She'd even chosen music to go with his meal, and although he'd never really thought jazz was his thing, the mellow strains of sax and piano had been the perfect go-with.

It was a big difference from the way he'd enjoyed dinner before—food that came out of a bag or the microwave, beer that came out of a longneck and some sport on TV. If someone had told Hogan a month ago that he'd be having dinner in a massive dining room at a table for twelve with a view of trees and town houses out his window instead of the neon sign for Taco Taberna across the street, he would have told that person to see a doctor about their hallucinations. He still couldn't believe this was his life now. He wasn't sure he ever would.

The moment he laid his fork on his plate, Chloe appeared to remove both from the table and set a cup of coffee in their place. Before she could escape again—somehow it always seemed to Hogan like she was trying to run from him—he stopped her.

"That was delicious," he said. "Thank you."

When she turned to face him, she looked surprised by his admission. "Of course it was delicious. It's my life's work to make it delicious." Seemingly as an afterthought, she added, "You're welcome."

When she started to turn away, Hogan stopped her again.

"So I realize now that *croque monsieur* is a ham and cheese sandwich, but what do you call those potatoes?"

When she turned around this time, her expression relayed nothing of what she might be thinking. She only gazed at him in silence for a minute—a minute where he was surprised to discover he was dying to know what she was thinking. Finally she said, "*Pommes frites.* The potatoes are called *pommes frites.*"

"And the green stuff? What was that?"

"*Salade de chou.*"

"Fancy," he said. "But wasn't it really just a ham and cheese sandwich, French fries and coleslaw?"

Her lips, freshly stained with her red lipstick, thinned a little. "To you? Yes. Now if you'll excuse me, your dessert—"

"Can wait a minute," he finished. "Sit down. We need to talk."

She didn't turn to leave again. But she didn't sit down, either. Mostly, she just stared at him through slitted eyes over the top of her glasses before pushing them into place again with the back of her hand. He remembered her doing that a couple of times earlier in the day. Maybe with what he was paying her now, she could afford to buy a pair of glasses that fit. Or, you know, eight hundred pairs of glasses that fit. He was paying her an awful lot.

He tried to gentle his tone. "Come on. Sit down. Please," he added.

"Was there a problem with your dinner?" she asked.

He shook his head. "It was a damned tasty ham and cheese sandwich."

He thought she would be offended that he relegated her creation—three times now—to something normally bought in a corner deli and wrapped in wax paper. Instead, she replied, "I wanted to break you in slowly. Tomorrow I'm making you *pot au feu.*"

"Which is?"

"To you? Beef stew."

"You don't think much of me or my palate, do you?"

"I have no opinion of either, Mr. Dempsey."

"Hogan," he corrected her. Again.

She continued as if he hadn't spoken. "I just happened to learn a few things about my new employer before starting work for him, and it's helped me plan menus that would appeal to him. Which was handy since the questionnaire I asked this particular employer to fill out was, shall we say, a bit lean on helpful information in that regard."

"Shouldn't I be the one doing that?" he asked. "Researching my potential employee before even offering the position?"

"Did you?" she asked.

He probably should have. But Gus Fiver's recommendation had been enough for him. Well, that and the fact that stealing her from Anabel would get the latter's attention.

"Uh…" he said eloquently.

She exhaled a resigned sigh then approached the table and pulled out a chair to fold herself into it, setting his empty plate before her for the time being.

"I know you grew up in a working-class neighborhood in Astoria," she said, "and that you're so new money, with so much of it, the Secret Service should be crawling into your shorts to make sure you're not printing the bills yourself. I know you've never traveled farther north than New Bedford, Massachusetts, to visit your grandparents or farther south than Ocean City, New Jersey, where you and your parents spent a week every summer at the Coral Sands Motel. I know you excelled at both hockey and football in high school and that you missed out on scholarships for both by *this much*, so you never went to college. I also know your favorite food is—" at this, she bit back a grimace "—taco meatloaf and that the only alcohol you imbibe is domestic beer. News flash. I will *not* be making taco meatloaf for you at any time."

The hell she wouldn't. Taco meatloaf was awesome. All he said, though, was, "How do you know all that? I mean, yeah, some of that stuff is probably on the internet, but not the stuff about my grandparents and the Coral Sands Motel."

"I would never pry into anyone's personal information on the internet or anywhere else," Chloe said, sounding genuinely stung that he would think otherwise.

"Then how—"

"Anabel told me all that about you after I gave her my two weeks' notice. I didn't ask," she hastened to clarify. "But when she found out it was you who hired me, and when she realized she couldn't afford to pay me more than you offered me, she became a little…perturbed."

Hogan grinned. He remembered Anabel *perturbed*. She never liked it much when she didn't get her way. "And she thought she could talk you out of coming to work for me by telling you what a mook I am, right?" he asked.

Chloe looked confused. "Mook?"

He chuckled. "Never mind."

Instead of being offended by what Anabel had told Chloe, Hogan was actually heartened by it, because it meant she remembered him well. It didn't surprise him she had said what she did. Anabel had never made a secret of her opinion that social divisions existed for a reason and should never be crossed—even if she had crossed them dozens of times to be with him when they were young. It was what she had been raised to believe and was as ingrained a part of her as Hogan's love for muscle cars was ingrained in him. Her parents, especially her father, had been adamant she would marry a man who was her social and financial equal, to the point that they'd sworn to cut her off socially and financially if she didn't. The Carlisle money was just that old and sacred. It was the *only* thing that could come between Hogan and Anabel. She'd made that clear, too. And when she went off to college and started dating a senator's son, well... Hogan had known it was over between them without her even having to tell him.

Except that she never actually told him it was over between them, and they'd still enjoyed the occasional hookup when she was home from school, in spite of the senator's son. Over the next few years, though, they finally did drift apart.

But Anabel never told him it was over.

That was why, even after she'd married the senator's son, Hogan had never stopped hoping that someday things would be different for them. And now his hope had paid off. Literally. The senator's son was gone, and there was no social or financial divide between him and Anabel anymore. The blood he was born with was just as blue as hers, and the money he'd inherited was just as old and moldy. Maybe he was still feeling his way in a world that was new to him, but he wasn't on the outside looking in anymore. Hell, he'd just drunk beer from a glass instead of a longneck. That was a major development for him. It wouldn't be long before he—

"Hang on," he said. "How does Anabel know I only drink domestic beer? I wasn't old enough to drink when I was with her."

"That part I figured out myself," Chloe said.

"There are some damned fine domestic beers being brewed these days, you know."

"There are. But what you had tonight was Belgian. Nice, wasn't it?"

Yeah, okay, it was. He would still be bringing home his Sam Adams on the weekends. *So there, Chloe Merlin.*

"Is everything you cook French?" he asked. He wasn't sure why he was prolonging a conversation neither of them seemed to want to have.

"Still angling for that taco meatloaf, are we?" she asked.

"I like pizza, too."

She flinched, but said nothing.

"And chicken pot pie," he threw in for good measure.

She expelled another one of those impatient sighs. "Fine. I can alter my menus. Some," she added meaningfully.

Hogan smiled. Upper hand. He had it. He wondered how long he could keep it.

"But yes, all of what I cook is French." She looked like she would add more to the comment, but she didn't.

So he tried a new tack. "Are you a native New Yorker?" Then he remembered she couldn't be a native New Yorker. She didn't know what a mook was.

"I was born and raised in New Albany, Indiana," she told him. Then, because she must have realized he was going to press her for more, she added, with clear reluctance, "I was raised by my grandmother because my parents…um…weren't able to raise me themselves. Mémée came here as a war bride after World War Two—her parents owned a bistro in Cherbourg—and she was the one who taught me to cook. I got my degree in Culinary Arts from Sullivan University in Louisville, which is a cool city, but the restaurant scene there is hugely competitive, and I wanted to open my own place."

"So you came to New York, where there's no competition for that kind of thing at all, huh?" He smiled, but Chloe didn't smile back.

He waited for her to explain how she had ended up in New York cooking for the One Percent instead of opening her own restaurant, but she must have thought she had come to the end of her story, because she didn't say anything else. For Hogan, though, her conclusion only jump-started a bunch of new questions in his brain. "So you wanted to open your own place, but you've been cooking for one person at a time for…how long?"

She met his gaze levelly. "For five years," she said.

He wondered if that was why she charged so much for her services and insisted on living on-site. Because she was saving up to open her own restaurant.

"Why no restaurant of your own by now?" he asked.

She hesitated for a short, but telling, moment.

"I changed my mind." She stood and picked up his plate. "I need to see to your dessert."

He wanted to ask her more about herself, but her posture made clear she was finished sharing. So instead, he asked, "What am I having?"

"*Glissade.*"

"Which is? To me?" he added before she could.

"Chocolate pudding."

And then she was gone. He turned in his chair to watch her leave and saw her crossing the gallery to the kitchen, her red plastic shoes whispering over the marble floor. He waited to see if she would look back, or even to one side. But she kept her gaze trained on the kitchen door, her step never slowing or faltering.

She was a focused one, Chloe Merlin. He wondered why. And he found himself wondering, too, if there was anything else—or anyone else—in her life besides cooking.

# Two

The day after she began working for Hogan Dempsey, Chloe returned from her early-afternoon grocery shopping to find him in the gallery between the kitchen and dining room. He was dressed in a different pair of battered jeans from the day before, and a different sweater, this one the color of a ripe avocado. He must not have heard her as she topped the last stair because he was gazing intently at one photograph in particular. It was possible that if she continued to not make a sound, he wouldn't see her as she slipped into the kitchen. Because she'd really appreciate it if Hogan didn't see her as she slipped into the kitchen.

In fact, she'd really appreciate it if Hogan never noticed her again.

She still didn't know what had possessed her to reveal so much about herself last night. She never told anyone about being raised by a grandmother instead of by parents, and she certainly never talked about the desire she'd once had to open a restaurant. That was a dream she abandoned a long time ago, and she would never revisit it again. Never. Yet within hours of meeting Hogan, she was telling him those things and more. It was completely unprofessional, and Chloe was, if nothing else, utterly devoted to her profession.

She gripped the tote bags in her hands more fiercely and stole a few more steps toward the kitchen. She was confident she didn't make a sound, but Hogan must have sensed her presence anyway and called out to her. Maybe she could pretend she didn't hear him. It couldn't be more than five or six more steps to the kitchen door. She might be able to make it.

"Chloe?" he said again.

Damn. Missed it by that much.

She turned to face him. "Yes, Mr. Dempsey?"

"Hogan," he told her again. "I don't like being called 'Mr. Dempsey.' It makes me uncomfortable. It's Hogan, okay?"

"All right," she agreed reluctantly. "What is it you need?"

When he'd called out to her, he'd sounded like he genuinely had something to ask her. Now, though, he only gazed at her in silence, looking much the way he had yesterday when he'd seemed so lost. And just as she had yesterday, Chloe had to battle the urge to go to him, to touch him, and to tell him not to worry, that everything would be all right. Not that she would ever tell him that. There were some things that could never be all right again. No one knew that better than Chloe did.

Thankfully, he quickly regrouped, pointing at the photo he'd been studying. "It's my mother," he said. "My biological mother," he quickly added. "I think I resemble her a little. What do you think?"

What Chloe thought was that she needed to start cooking. Immediately. Instead, she set her bags on the floor and made her way across the gallery toward him and the photo.

His mother didn't resemble him *a little*, she saw. His mother resembled him a lot. In fact, looking at her was like looking at a female Hogan Dempsey.

"Her name was Susan Amherst," he said. "She was barely sixteen when she had me."

Even though Chloe truly didn't engage in gossip, she hadn't been able to avoid hearing the story of Susan Amherst over the last several weeks. It was all the Park Avenue crowd had talked about since the particulars of Philip Amherst's estate were made public, from the tearooms where society matriarchs congregated to the kitchens where their staff toiled. How Susan Amherst, a prominent young society deb in the early '80s, suddenly decided not to attend Wellesley after her graduation from high school a year early, and instead took a year off to "volunteer overseas." There had been talk at the time that she was pregnant and that her ultra-conservative, extremely image-conscious parents wanted to hide her condition. Rumors swirled that they sent her to live with relatives upstate and had the baby adopted immediately after its birth. But the talk about young Susan died down as soon as another scandal came along, and life went on. Even for the Amhersts. Susan returned to her rightful place in her parents' home the following spring and started college the next year. For all anyone knew, she really had spent months "volunteering overseas."

Until Hogan showed up three decades later and stirred up the talk again.

"You and she resemble each other very much," Chloe said. And because Susan's parents were in the photograph, as well, she added, "You resemble your grandfather, too." She stopped herself before adding that Philip Amherst had been a very handsome man.

"My grandfather's attorney gave me a letter my grandfather wrote when he changed his will to leave his estate to me." Hogan's voice revealed nothing of what he might be feeling, even though there must be a tsunami of feeling in a statement like that. "The adoption was a private one at a time when sealed records stayed sealed, so he couldn't find me before he died.

"Not that I got the impression from his letter that he actually *wanted* to find me before he died," he hastened to add. Oh, yes. Definitely a tsunami of feeling. "It took a bunch of legal proceedings to get the records opened so the estate could pass to me. Anyway, in his letter, he said Susan didn't want to put me up for adoption. That she wanted to raise me herself. She even named me. Travis. Travis Amherst." He chuckled, but there wasn't an ounce of humor in the sound. "I mean, can you see me as a Travis Amherst?"

Actually, Chloe could. Hogan Dempsey struck her as a man who could take any form and name he wanted. Travis Amherst of the Upper East Side would have been every bit as dynamic and compelling as Hogan Dempsey of Queens. He just would have been doing it in a different arena.

"Not that it matters," he continued. "My grandparents talked Susan out of keeping me because she was so young—she was only fifteen when she got pregnant. They convinced her it was what was best for her and me both."

He looked at the photo again. In it, Susan Amherst looked to be in her thirties. She was wearing a black cocktail dress and was flanked by her parents on one side and a former, famously colorful, mayor of New York on the other. In the background were scores of people on a dance floor and, behind them, an orchestra. Whatever the event was, it seemed to be festive. Susan, however, wasn't smiling. She obviously didn't feel very festive.

"My mother never told anyone who my father was," Hogan continued. "But my grandfather said he thought he was one of the servants' kids that Susan used to sneak out with. From some of the other stuff he said, I think he was more worried about that than he was my mother's age." He paused. "Not that that matters now, either."

Chloe felt his gaze fall on her again. When she looked at him, his eyes were dark with a melancholy sort of longing.

"Of course it matters," she said softly. "Your entire life would have been different if you had grown up Travis Amherst instead of Hogan Dempsey." And because she couldn't quite stop herself, she added, "It's…difficult…when life throws something at you that you never could have seen coming. Especially when you realize it's going to change *every*thing. Whatever you're feeling, Hogan, they're legitimate feelings, and they deserve to be acknowledged. You don't have to pretend it doesn't matter. It matters," she repeated adamantly. "It matters a lot."

Too late, she realized she had called him Hogan. Too late, she realized she had spilled something out of herself onto him again and made an even bigger mess than she had last night. Too late, she realized she couldn't take any of it back.

But Hogan didn't seem to think she'd made a mess. He seemed to be grateful for what she'd said. "Thanks," he told her.

And because she couldn't think of anything else to say, she replied automatically, "You're welcome."

She was about to return to the kitchen—she really, really, really did need to get cooking—but he started talking again, his voice wistful, his expression sober.

"I can't imagine what my life would have been like growing up as Travis Amherst. I would have had to go to some private school where I probably would have played soccer and lacrosse instead of football and hockey. I would have gone to college. I probably would have majored in business or finance and done one of those study-abroads in Europe. By now Travis Amherst would be saddled with some office job, wearing pinstripes by a designer whose name Hogan Dempsey wouldn't even recognize." He shook his head, clearly baffled by what might have been. "The thought of having to work at a job like that instead of working at the garage is…" He inhaled deeply and released the breath slowly. "It's just… A job like that would suffocate me. But Travis Amherst probably would have loved it."

"Possibly," Chloe said. "But maybe not. Travis

might have liked working with his hands, too. It's impossible to know for sure."

"And pointless to play 'what if,' I know," Hogan agreed. "What's done is done. And the idea that I would have never known my mom and dad or have the friends I've had all my life… The thought of all the memories that live in my head being completely different…"

Chloe winced inwardly at the irony of their situation. They both grieved for the unknown. But with him, it was a past that hadn't happened, and for her, it was a future that would never be.

"I need to cook," she told him. She pushed her glasses into place with the back of her hand and took a step backward. "I'm sorry, but…" She took another step back. "I need to cook. If you'll excuse me…"

"Sure," he said. "No problem." He didn't sound like there wasn't a problem, though. He sounded really confused.

That made two of them.

When Chloe turned to head back to the kitchen, she saw Mrs. Hennessey topping the last stair. Hogan's housekeeper reminded her of her grandmother in a lot of ways. She wore the same boxy house dresses in the same muted colors and always kept her fine white hair twisted into a flawless chignon at her nape. She was no-nonsense and professional, the way Chloe was. At least, the way Chloe was before she came to work for Hogan. The way she knew she had to be again if she wanted to keep working here.

And she did want to keep working here. For some reason. A reason she wasn't ready to explore. It was sure to be good, whatever it was.

Mrs. Hennessey announced to the room at large, "There's an Anabel Carlisle downstairs to see you. I showed her to the salon."

That seemed to snap Hogan out of his preoccupation with what might have been and pull him firmly into the here and now. "Anabel is here? Tell her I'll be right down."

"No, Mr. Dempsey, she's here to see Ms. Merlin."

Hogan's jaw dropped a little at that. But all he said was, "Hogan, Mrs. Hennessey. Please call me Hogan." Then he looked at Chloe. "Guess she refigured her budget and wants to hire you back."

Chloe should have been delighted by the idea. Not only did it mean more money coming in, but it also meant she would be free of Hogan Dempsey and his damnable heartache-filled eyes. She should be flying down the stairs to tell Anabel that she'd love to come back to work for her and would pack her bags this instant. Instead, for some reason, she couldn't move. "Tell Anabel we'll be right down," Hogan told Mrs. Hennessey.

The housekeeper nodded and went back down the stairs. Chloe stood still. Hogan gazed at her curiously.

"Don't you want to hear what she has to say?"

Chloe nodded. She did. She did want to hear what Anabel had to say. But she really needed to cook. Cooking was something she could control. Cooking filled her head with flavors and fragrances, with methods and measurements. Cooking restored balance to the universe. And Chloe could really use some balance right now.

"Well then, let's go find out," Hogan said.

Chloe looked at him again. And was immediately sorry. Because now he looked happy and eager and excited. And a happy Hogan was far more overwhelming, and far more troubling, than a conflicted one. A happy Hogan reminded her of times and places—and people—that had made her happy, too. And those thoughts, more than anything, were the very reason she needed to cook.

Hogan couldn't understand why Chloe looked so unhappy at the thought of seeing Anabel. Then again, Chloe hadn't really looked happy about anything since he met her. He'd never encountered anyone so serious. Even cooking, which she constantly said she wanted to do, didn't really seem to bring her any joy.

Then he remembered she'd never actually said she *wanted* to cook. She always said she *needed* to. For most people, that was probably a minor distinction.

He was beginning to suspect that, for Chloe, there was nothing minor about it at all.

"C'mon," he told her. "Let's go see what Anabel wants." And then, because she was standing close enough for him to do it, he leaned over and nudged her shoulder gently with his.

He might as well have jabbed her with a red-hot poker, the way she lurched away from him at the contact. She even let out a soft cry of protest and lifted a hand to her shoulder, as if he'd struck her there.

"I'm sorry," he immediately apologized, even though he had no idea what he needed to apologize for. "I didn't mean to…"

What? Touch her? Of course he meant to touch her. The same way he would have touched any one of his friends, male or female, in an effort to coax them out of their funk. People always nudged each other's shoulders. Most people wouldn't have even noticed the gesture. Chloe looked as if she'd been shot.

"It's okay," she said, still rubbing her shoulder, not looking like it was okay at all.

Not knowing what else he could say, he extended his arm toward the stairs to indicate she should precede him down. With one last, distressed look at him, she did. He kept his distance as he followed her because she seemed to need it, but also because it gave him a few more seconds to prepare for Anabel. He'd known he would run into her at some point—

hell, he'd planned on it—but he'd figured it would be at some social function where there would be a lot of people around, and he'd have plenty of time to plan. He hadn't thought she would come to his house, even if it was to see someone other than him.

What Mrs. Hennessey called a "salon," Hogan thought of as a big-ass living room. The walls were paneled in maple, and a massive Oriental rug covered most of the green marble floor. A fireplace on one wall had a mantel that was dotted with wooden model ships, and it was flanked by brown leather chairs—a matching sofa was pushed against the wall opposite.

Three floor-to-ceiling arched windows looked out onto a courtyard in back of the house, and it was through one of those that Anabel Carlisle stood looking, with her back to them. Either she hadn't heard them come in, or she, too, was giving herself a few extra seconds to prepare. All Hogan could tell was that the black hair that used to hang in straight shafts to the middle of her back was short now, cut nearly to her chin.

And her wardrobe choices were a lot different, too. He remembered her trying to look like a secondhand gypsy, even though she'd probably spent hundreds of dollars in Fifth Avenue boutiques on everything she wore. Today's outfit had likely set her back even more, despite merely consisting of sedate gray pants and sweater. But both showcased lush curves she hadn't had as a teenager, so maybe they were worth the extra expense.

As if he'd spoken his appraisal out loud, Anabel suddenly spun around. Although she looked first at Chloe, she didn't seem to be surprised by Hogan's presence. But whether the smile on her face was for him or his chef, he couldn't have said. "Hogan," she said in the same throaty voice he remembered. God, he'd always loved her voice. "Good to see you."

"You, too, Anabel. How have you been?"

She began to walk toward where he and Chloe stood in the doorway. She still moved the way she used to, all grace and elegance and style. He'd always loved watching her move. She was just as gorgeous now as she'd been when they were kids. Even more, really, because she'd ditched the heavy eye makeup and dark lipstick she used to wear, so her natural beauty shone through. Strangely, the lack of makeup only made her blue eyes seem even bluer than he remembered them and her mouth even fuller and lusher.

He waited for the splash of heat that had always rocked his midsection whenever he saw her, and for the hitch of breath that had always gotten caught in his chest. But neither materialized. He guessed he'd outgrown reactions like that.

"I imagine you've already heard most of the highlights about how I've been," she said as she drew nearer. "My divorce was the talk of the town until you showed up." She smiled again, but there was only good humor and maybe a little nostalgia in the gesture. "I should actually probably thank you for that."

"You're welcome," he said, smiling back.

It really was good to see her. She really did look great. So what if his heart wasn't pumping like the V-8 in a Challenger Hellcat, the way he would have thought it would be. People grew up. Hormones settled down.

With one last look at Hogan she turned her attention to Chloe.

"I want you to come back to work for me," she said, straight to the point. "I can pay you three percent more than Hogan offered you."

Hogan looked at Chloe. She still seemed shellshocked from whatever the hell had happened between them in the gallery. She glanced at Hogan, then back at Anabel, but said nothing.

Cagey, he thought. She was probably thinking if Anabel was offering three percent, she could get more from Hogan. Fine. Whatever it took to keep Chloe on, Hogan would pay it. Especially if it meant Anabel might come around again.

"I'll raise your salary five percent," he told her.

Anabel looked at him, her lips parted in surprise. Or something. Then she looked back at Chloe. "I can go six percent," she said coolly. "And you can have the entire month of August off, with pay."

Again, Chloe looked at Hogan, then back at Anabel. Again, she remained silent.

"Eight percent," Hogan countered.

Now Anabel narrowed her eyes at him in a way he remembered well. It was her *I'll-get-what-I-want-or-else* look. She always wore it right before he agreed to spring for tickets for whatever band happened to be her favorite at the time, or whatever restaurant was her favorite, or whatever whatever was her favorite. Then again, she'd always thanked him with hours and hours of hot *I-love-you-so-much* sex. Well, okay, maybe not hours and hours. He hadn't been the most controlled lover back in the day. But it had for sure been hot.

Anabel didn't up her salary offer this time, but she told Chloe, "And I'll give you the suite of rooms that face the park."

Chloe opened her mouth to reply, but Hogan stopped her with another counteroffer. "I'll raise your pay ten percent," he said. He didn't add anything about a better room or more time off. Not just because she already had a damned suitable room and more time off than the average person could ever hope to have, but because something told him money was way more important to Chloe than anything else.

What she needed the money for, Hogan couldn't imagine. But it was her salary that had been the most important part of her contract, her salary that lured her from one employer to another. Chloe Merlin wanted money. Lots of it.

For a third time she looked at Hogan, then at Anabel. "I'm sorry, Anabel," she said. "Unless you can offer to pay me more than Mr. ...." She threw another glance Hogan's way, this one looking even more edgy than the others. Then she turned so that her entire body was facing Anabel. "Unless you can offer me more than...that...I'm afraid I'll have to remain here."

There was a brief expectant pause, and when Anabel only shook her head, Chloe made her way to the doorway. "I'll draw up a rider for my contract and have it for you this evening," she said to Hogan as she started back up the stairs.

And then she was gone, without saying goodbye to either of them.

"She is such an odd duck," Anabel said when Chloe was safely out of earshot.

There was nothing derogatory in her tone, just a matter-of-factness that had been there even when they were teenagers. She wasn't condemning Chloe, just stating the truth. His chef was pretty unique.

"But worth every penny," she added with a sigh. She smiled again. "More pennies than I can afford to pay her. Obviously, she's working for someone who's out of my league."

Hogan shook his head. "Other way around, Anabel. You were always out of my league. You said so yourself. More than once, if I remember."

She winced at the comment, even though he hadn't meant it maliciously. He'd learned to be matter-of-fact from her. "I was a dumb kid when we dated, Hogan," she told him. "I was so full of myself back then. I said a lot of things I shouldn't have."

"Nah," he told her. "You never said anything I wasn't thinking myself. You were right. We came from two different worlds."

"Even so, that didn't give me the right to be such an elitist. My parents just taught me their philosophy well. It took me years to figure out I was wrong."

Now there was a loaded statement. Wrong about what? Wrong about the prejudice her parents taught her? Wrong about some of the comments she'd made? Wrong about their social circles never mixing? Wrong about leaving him for the senator's son?

Probably better not to ask for clarification. Not yet anyway. He and Anabel had rushed headlong into their relationship when they were kids. The first time they'd had sex was within days of meeting, and they'd almost never met without having sex. He'd sometimes wondered if maybe they'd gone slower, things would have worked out differently. This time he wasn't going to hurry it. This time he wanted to do it right.

"So how have you been?" she asked him. "How

are your folks? I still think about your mom's Toll House cookies from time to time."

"My folks are gone," he told her. "Mom passed five years ago. Dad went two years later. Cancer. Both of them."

She looked stricken by the news. She lifted a hand to his shoulder and gave it a gentle squeeze. "Oh, Hogan, I am so sorry. I had no idea."

He covered her hand with his. "You couldn't have known. And thanks."

For a moment neither of them said anything, then Anabel dropped her hand. She crossed her arms over her midsection and looked at the door. Hogan told himself to ask her something about herself, but he didn't want to bring up her divorce, even if she didn't seem to be any the worse for wear from it. Her folks, he figured, were probably the same as always. Maybe a little more likely to invite him into their home than they were fifteen years ago, but then again, maybe not.

But for the life of him, he couldn't think of a single thing to say.

"I should probably get going," she said. "I have a thing tonight. My aunt and uncle are in town. We're meeting at the Rainbow Room." She expelled a sound that was a mixture of affection and irritation. "They always want to meet at the Rainbow Room. Which is great, but really, I wish they'd expand their repertoire a bit. Try Per Se or Morimoto sometime. Or Le Turtle. I love that place."

Okay, she'd just given Hogan the perfect opening. Three different restaurants she obviously loved. All he had to do was say, *What a coincidence, Anabel, I've been wanting to expand my repertoire, too. Why don't you and I have dinner at one of those places? You pick.* And they'd be off. For some reason, though, he just couldn't get the words to move out of his brain and into his mouth.

Not that Anabel had seemed to be angling for an invitation, because she didn't miss a beat when she continued, "Ah, well. Old habits die hard, I guess."

Which was another statement that could have been interpreted in more ways than one. Was she talking about her aunt and uncle now, and their dining habits? Or was she talking about her and Hogan, and how she still maybe had a thing for him? It didn't used to be this hard to read her. And why the hell didn't he just ask her out to see how she responded?

"It was good to see you again, Hogan," she said as she took a step in retreat. "I'm glad Philip Amherst's attorneys found you," she continued as she took another. "Maybe our paths will cross again before long."

"Maybe so," he said, finding his voice.

She lifted a hand in farewell then turned and made her way toward the exit. Just as she was about to disappear into the hallway, Hogan thought of something to ask her.

"Hey, Anabel."

She halted and turned back around, but said nothing.

"If I'd grown up an Amherst…" Hogan began. "I mean, if you'd met me as, say, a guy named Travis Amherst from the Upper East Side who went to some private school and played lacrosse and was planning to go to Harvard after graduation, instead of meeting me as Hogan Dempsey, grease monkey…"

She smiled again, this one definitely nostalgic. "Travis Amherst wouldn't have been you, Hogan. He would have been like a million other guys I knew. If I'd met you as Travis Amherst, I never would have bothered with you."

"You bothered with the senator's son," he reminded her. "And he had to have been like those million other guys."

"Yeah, he was. And look how that turned out."

Good point.

"You take care, Hogan."

"You, too, Anabel."

She threw him one last smile, lifted a hand in goodbye then turned around again and made her way down the hall. He heard her footsteps gradually fade away, then heard Mrs. Hennessey open and close the front door for her. Then, as quickly as she'd shown up in his life again, Anabel was gone.

And as the front door clicked shut behind her, it occurred to Hogan that, just like last time, she never actually told him goodbye.

# Three

Although Chloe had Sundays and Mondays off, she rarely used them to relax. She generally went out in the morning and often didn't return until nearly dark—or even after—but the hours in between were almost always devoted to things related to cooking. Sometimes she explored new shops or revisited old favorites to familiarize herself with what they had in stock or to pick up a few essentials. Sometimes she sat in on lectures or classes that addressed new methods or trends in cooking. Sometimes she checked out intriguing restaurants to see what was on their menus that she might adapt for her own. Sometimes she attended tastings of cheeses, charcuterie, beers or wines.

It was to one of the last that she was headed out late Monday afternoon when she ran into Hogan, who was coming in the back door. She'd been exceptionally good at avoiding him since last week when Anabel had tried to hire her back—the same afternoon she'd shared those odd few moments with Hogan in the gallery that had ended with her completely overreacting when he nudged her shoulder with his.

She still wanted to slap herself for recoiling from him the way she had. There had been nothing inappropriate in his gesture. On the contrary, he'd obviously been trying to be friendly. There was a time when Chloe loved having her shoulder nudged in exactly that same way by…friends. It had just been so unexpected, that was all. Especially coming from someone who wasn't…a friend.

And, okay, it had also been a long time since someone had touched her with anything resembling friendship. It had been a long time since anyone had touched her at all. She went out of her way to avoid physical contact these days. With everyone. It just wasn't professional. Among other things.

It was those *among other things* that especially came into play with Hogan. Because even an innocent touch like a nudge to the shoulder felt… Well. Not innocent. Not on her end anyway. Not since it had been so long since anyone had touched her with anything resembling friendship. Or something.

Which was why she had been super careful not to let it happen again. Since that afternoon, dinner every night had been nothing but serving, identifying and describing Hogan's food. No more sitting down at his table. No more spilling her guts. And certainly no more touching. She was his chef. He was her employer. Period. Thankfully, he finally got the message, because after three or four nights of her sidestepping every question he asked about her by replying with something about the food instead, he'd finally stopped asking.

At least, that was what she'd thought until she saw him today. Because the minute he stepped inside he smiled that damnably charming smile of his and said, with much friendliness, "Chloe, hi. Where you going?"

It was the kind of question, spoken with the kind of expression that was almost always followed by *Can I come, too*? He just looked so earnest and appealing and sweet, and something inside Chloe that had been cold and hard and discordant for a very long time began to grow warm and soft and agreeable.

*Stop that*, she told that part of herself. *Stop it right now.*

But that part wouldn't listen, because it just kept feeling better. So she did her best to ignore it.

"Must be someplace really nice," he added. "'Cause you look really nice."

Had she thought that part of her was only growing warm? Well, now it was spontaneously combusting. The man's smile just had that effect. As did the fact that he was wearing garage-issue coveralls streaked with machine oil, an outfit that should have been unappealing—and on anyone else in her social sphere, it probably would have been—but only served to make Hogan look even more handsome.

She'd always found the working-class hero too damnably attractive. Men who worked with their hands *and* their brains could, at the end of the day, point to something concrete that was actually useful to society and say *Hey, I did that with my bare hands.* Inevitably, that always made her think about what else a man like that could do with his bare hands—especially at the end of the day. And, inevitably, she always remembered. Men like that could make a woman feel wonderful.

She pushed her glasses up with the back of her hand—it was a nervous gesture, she knew, but dammit, she was nervous—and, without thinking, told him, "You look really nice, too."

Only when he chuckled did she realize what she had said and immediately wished she could take back the words.

But Hogan shrugged off the comment. "No, I look like I've spent the better part of the afternoon under a 1957 Mercedes-Benz Three Hundred SL Gullwing that belonged to my grandfather. Which I have been. *You* look really nice. So where you going?"

It was nice of him to say so, but Chloe was the epitome of plain in a black pencil skirt, white shirt, claret-colored cardigan and black flats—all of which she had owned since college—with her hair piled on top of her head, the way it always was.

"Thank you," she made herself say, even though she was uncomfortable with the compliment. "I'm going to a wine-tasting."

She thought the announcement would put an end to any idea he might have about joining her. She was still serving him beer with his dinner—though he had certainly expanded his horizons there—and was hoping to find a few wines at this tasting today that might break him in easily.

"Sounds like fun," he said. Even though he didn't sound like he thought it was fun. In spite of that, he added, "Want some company?"

Of course she didn't want company. Chloe hadn't wanted company for years. Six years, in fact. Six years and eight months, to be precise. Six years, eight months, two weeks and three days, to be even more precise.

"I mean, knowing about wine," Hogan continued, "that could help me in the Anabel department, right? I need to know this stuff if I'm going to be moving in her circles. Make a good impression and all that."

He wasn't wrong, Chloe thought. She knew for

a fact that Anabel Carlisle knew and enjoyed her wines. She could invite Hogan to come along, if for no other reason than that. And what other reason could there be?

Even so, she hedged, "Actually, I—"

But Hogan cut her off. "Great. Gimme ten minutes to clean up and change clothes. Be right back."

She was so stunned by his response that it took her a minute to react. She spun around and said, "But—"

But she knew he wouldn't hear her, because he was already pounding up the stairs.

She told herself to leave before he got back and explain her disappearance later by saying she'd assumed he was joking so went her merry way. She really didn't want company today. Or any day. So why didn't she slip out the door and make her way up 67th Street to Madison Avenue, where she could lose herself in both the crowd and the sunny October afternoon? Why did her feet seem to be nailed to the floor? More to the point, why did a part of her actually kind of like the prospect of spending the rest of the afternoon with Hogan?

She was still contemplating those questions and a host of others when he reappeared ten minutes later. The man was nothing if not punctual. And also incredibly handsome. So far she'd seen him in nothing but jeans and sweaters and greasy coveralls, but, having clearly taken a cue from her own outfit, he now wore a pair of khaki trousers, a pinstriped ox-ford and a chocolate-colored blazer. And in place of his usual battered work boots were a pair of plain leather mocs—not quite as well-worn as the boots, but still obviously, ah…of a certain age. Just like everything else he had on.

How could a man have inherited as much money as Hogan had and not have spent at least some of it on new shoes and clothes? Then again, who was she to judge? The last time Chloe bought a new ar-ticle of clothing for herself, it had been for… Well, it wasn't important what she'd bought the dress for. It had been six years since she'd worn it. Six years, eight months, two weeks and six days, to be precise. And she'd gotten rid of it soon after.

As Hogan began to walk toward her, heat bloomed in her midsection again, only this time it was joined by a funny sort of shimmying that only made it more enjoyable.

*No!* she immediately told herself. *Not enjoyable.* What she was feeling was…something else. Some-thing that had nothing to do with enjoyment.

As he drew nearer, she noticed he hadn't man-aged quite as well with his grooming as he had his clothing. There was a tiny streak of oil over his eye-brow that he'd missed.

"All set," he said when he stopped in front of her.

"Not quite," she told him.

His expression fell. "I've never been to a wine-tasting. Should I change my clothes?"

She shook her head. "No, your outfit is fine. It's a casual event. It's just that…"

He was within touching distance now, and she had to battle the urge to lift a hand to his face and wipe away the oil herself. The gesture would have been no more inappropriate than his nudging of her shoulder had been last week. For some reason, though, the thought of touching him in such a way felt no less innocent than that one had.

So instead, she pointed at his eyebrow and said, "You missed a spot of grease there. Over your left eyebrow."

He swiped the side of his hand over the place she indicated…and missed the streak by millimeters.

"It's still there," she said.

He tried again, this time with the heel of his palm. But again, he missed it by *that much*.

"Still there," she said again.

He uttered an impatient sound. "Do you mind getting it for me?"

He might as well have asked her if she minded picking him up and heaving him out the window. Did he really not understand that physical contact was a physical impossibility for her after the way she'd overreacted to being touched by him last week? Were they going to have to endure another awkward moment to make that clear?

Strangely, though, the thought of touching Hogan now was slightly less…difficult…than it should have been. Resigning herself, she reached toward his face. Hogan's gaze hitched with hers, making it impossible for her to untether herself. Those brown, brown eyes, richer than truffles and sweeter than muscovado, made her pulse leap wildly, and her mouth go dry. Finally, finally, her hand made contact with his face, the pad of her index finger skimming lightly over his brow.

Her first attempt to wipe away the smudge was as fruitless as his had been—not surprising, since she was barely touching him. She tried again, drawing her thumb over his skin this time—his warm, soft skin—and that was a bit more successful. But still, the stain lingered. So she dragged her thumb across it again, once, twice, three times, until at last, the spot disappeared.

She didn't realize until that moment how her breathing had escalated while she was touching him, or how hot her entire body had become. Her face, she knew, was flushed, because she could feel the heat in her cheeks, and her hand felt as if it had caught fire. Worse, her fingers were still stroking Hogan's forehead, lightly and idly, clearly not to clean up a speck of oil, but simply because she enjoyed the feel of a man's skin under her fingertips and didn't want to stop touching him yet. It had been so long since Chloe had touched a man this way. So long since she had felt the simple pleasure of warmth and strength and vitality against her skin. Even a fingertip.

Worst of all, Hogan seemed to realize exactly what she was feeling. His face was a little flushed, too, and his pupils had expanded to nearly eclipse the dark brown of his irises. Seemingly without thinking, he covered her hand with his and gently removed it. But instead of letting it go after maneuvering it between them, which she had thought he would do—which he really should do—he held on to it, stroking his thumb lightly over her palm.

The warmth in her midsection went supernova at that, rushing heat to her every extremity. So acute was the sensation that she actually cried out—softly enough that she hoped he might not have heard her... except she knew right off he did. She knew because he finally severed his gaze from hers...only to let it fall to her mouth instead.

For one insane moment she thought he was going to kiss her. She even turned her head in a way that would keep her glasses from being a hindrance, the way she used to when— The way a person did when they knew something like that was about to happen. That was just how far she had allowed her desire to go. No, not desire, she immediately corrected herself. Appetite. Instinct. Drive. It had been too long since she'd enjoyed the sexual release every human being craved. Hogan was a very attractive man. Of course her body would respond to him the way it did. It was a matter of hormones and chemistry. There was nothing more to it than that.

Not that that wasn't more than enough.

He still hadn't released her hand, so, with much reluctance, she disengaged it herself and took a giant step backward. Then she took a breath, releasing it slowly to ease her pulse back to its normal rhythm and return her brain to its normal thoughts.

"There," she said softly. "All better."

She hoped he would think she was only talking about the removal of the oil streak from his face. But *all better* referred to herself, too. Her physical self, anyway. The emotional parts of her, though...

Well. Chloe knew she would never be *all* better. Not with so much of herself missing. But she was better now than she had been a few minutes ago, when touching Hogan had made so much of her feel so alive. That feeling was just a cruel ruse. She knew she would never feel alive again.

"All better," she tried again, forcefully enough this time that she sounded as if she actually believed it. "We should get going," she added. "We don't want to be late."

Hogan watched Chloe escape through the back door, his hand still hanging in the air between them. And he wondered, *What the hell just happened?* One minute he was asking her to wipe away a smudge of grease—an action that should have taken less than a second and been about as consequential as opening a jar of peanut butter—and the next, they were staring at each other, breathing as hard as they would have been if they'd just had sex. Really good sex, too.

His hand was even trembling, he noted as he forced himself to move it back to his side. And his whole body was hot, as if she'd run her fingers over every inch of him, instead of just his forehead. What the hell was up with that? The only person who was supposed to be making his hands shake and his skin hot was Anabel. Certainly not a near-stranger with a chip on her shoulder the size of the Brooklyn Bridge.

He gave his head a good shake to clear it. Then he made his feet move forward to follow Chloe, who had already gone through the back door. Outside on 67th Street, she was standing near a tree with her back to him, her face in profile as she gazed toward Madison Avenue—though she didn't look as if she was in any hurry to get anywhere. In fact, her expression was kind of distant and dreamy, as if it wasn't tasting wine she was thinking about, but tasting…uh…something else instead.

Hogan shoved the thought away. He had to be imagining things. Chloe Merlin had made it clear that she wanted to keep her distance from him, physically, mentally, emotionally, spiritually and every other-*ly* there was. Ever since that day last week when she'd reeled away from him in the gallery, she'd been professional to a fault. Every effort he'd made to get to know her better—because he always wanted to know a person better who was working for him, the same way he knew the guys who worked for him at the garage—had fallen flat.

Then again, he'd never met anyone like Chloe, so maybe it was just because of that.

By the time he drew alongside her on the street, she was back to her regular cool composure. When she looked at him now, it was with the same sort of detachment she always did. Her red-lipsticked mouth was flat, and she straightened her glasses with her fingers this time, instead of the back of her hand, a much less anxious gesture than usual. But he still couldn't quite forget that erotic little sound of surrender that had escaped her when he dragged his thumb along the inside of her palm. It would be a long time before he forgot about that.

"We're going to a new restaurant on Madison Avenue, just around the corner from sixty-seventh," she told him. "*L'Artichaut.* They don't actually open until next week, so it will be nice to have a little sneak peek in addition to the wine-tasting."

It suddenly occurred to Hogan that there might be a charge for him to participate. "Is it okay if you show up with someone? I mean, I have my wallet, but I don't have a lot of cash on me."

It was something he might have said in the past, when not having cash on him was a fairly regular occurrence. Saying something like that now, in light of his new financial situation, made him think he sounded like he was expecting Chloe to pick up the tab for him.

"There's no charge," she said. "It's by invitation. And mine included a plus-one. I just didn't, um, have a plus-one to invite."

Wow. She really was a Park Avenue sensation if she got invited to stuff like this. Then the second part of her statement registered. And made him a lot happier than it should have.

"I hope you don't mind having one now," he said.

"It's fine," she told him. But she still didn't sound like it was.

"Now that all the legalities of inheriting my grandfather's estate have been settled, it's kind of hard for me to keep busy, you know? I mean, I don't really have to work anymore, and, as much as I liked working in the garage, I thought I'd like not working more. Isn't that what everyone wants? Even people who like their jobs? To not have to get up every day and go to work?"

"I don't know," she said. "Is that what everyone wants?"

Well, everyone except, apparently, Chloe Merlin. Then again, she'd never said she liked her work. She said she needed it. He still wanted to know what the difference was. "*I* always thought it was," he said. "I started working for a paycheck in my dad's garage when I was fourteen, cleaning up and manning the cash register and running errands until I was old enough to work on the cars. When I was in high school, I worked another job, too, at a market up the street from us, delivering groceries."

Because it had taken the income from two jobs to keep Anabel in the style to which she was accustomed. Not that Hogan regretted a bit of it. She'd been worth every extra minute on his time cards.

The point was that he'd been working hard for more than two-thirds of his life. When Gus Fiver told him how much money he had now, Hogan had realized he could sleep late every morning and stay up late every night and enjoy a million different pursuits. Problem was, he wasn't much of a night owl—he liked getting up early. And he didn't really have any pursuits. Not yet. He hadn't even been away from his job for two weeks, and already, he was restless.

"I don't understand how the idle rich handle being idle," he said. "It feels weird to have all this money I didn't work for. I don't want to be one of those people who gets everything handed to them, you know? I need to figure out a way to earn my place in the world."

"Some wealthy people who don't work keep themselves busy by finding causes to support and raising money to help them. You could become a philanthropist."

He shook his head. "I'd rather just have someone tell me who needs something and write them a check." Which was something he'd actually started doing already. "There's nothing wrong with charity work," he hurried to add. "It's just not my thing. I'm not comfortable asking people for money, even if the money's not for me."

"But you are comfortable giving it away."

"Well, yeah. It's not like I need it. Just the income I get from my grandfather's investments has me set for life. Not only do I have that incredible house," he added, jabbing a thumb over his shoulder toward the place they'd just left, "but he left me three other houses to boot. The guy had four houses. Who needs that many?" Before she could answer—not that the question had really required an answer—he added, "And he collected cars. There are four parked under the town house and another eight in a storage facility in New Jersey. Not to mention another ten at his other houses. Twenty-two cars. Hell, even I think that's too many, and I've always wondered what it would be like to collect cars."

She almost smiled at that. Almost. It didn't quite make it into her eyes, though. Still, he guessed hearing some mook complain about having too many houses and cars was pretty funny. Her reaction made him feel better. Maybe they could get back on solid, if weird, ground again.

"So that was what you were doing this afternoon?" she asked. "Looking at the ones parked at the house?"

He nodded. "Yeah. They're in incredible condition. Maybe Philip Amherst wasn't a huge success in the father and grandfather departments, but the guy knew wheels. In addition to the Merc Gullwing, there's a 1961 Ferrari Spyder, a 1956 Maserati Berlinetta, and, just when I thought the guy was going to be one of those European snobs, I pull the cover off this incredible 1970 Chevy Chevelle SS 427 in absolute mint condition that's—"

He stopped midsentence, because Chloe was looking at him now with an actual, honest-to-God smile on her face, one that had reached her eyes this time, and the sight nearly knocked the breath out of his lungs. He'd been thinking all this time that she was cute. Quirky, but cute. But when she smiled the way she was smiling now, she was... She was a... She was an absolute... Wow. Really, really...wow.

But all he could manage to say was, "What's so funny?"

She looked ahead again. "I think you've found your purpose."

"What? Collecting cars?" he asked. "No, that's too much. I'm already having trouble justifying keeping them all."

"Then maybe you could do something else with cars," she suggested. "Start designing your own line."

He shook his head. "I don't have that kind of talent."

"Then invest in someone who does."

He started to shoot down that idea, too, but stopped. That actually wasn't a bad idea. He even already knew somebody he could put some money behind. The daughter of one of the guys who worked at the garage. She was still in high school, but the kid knew cars inside and out, and had some great ideas for what to do with them. No way could her parents afford to send her to college. But Hogan could. And there were probably dozens of kids like her in New York...

But he still needed to figure out what to do with himself. Investing in the future generation was great and all that, but Hogan needed a purpose, too. He'd worked with his hands all his life. He just couldn't see himself never working with them again.

Chloe halted, and Hogan realized they were standing in front of their destination. Looked like, for now, at least, what he would be doing was spending a few hours in a French restaurant tasting wine he knew nothing about. A couple of months ago the idea of doing something like that would have made him want to stick needles in his eyes. Today, though, it felt like a good way to spend the time.

He looked at Chloe again, at how the afternoon sun brought out sparks of silver in her white-blond hair and how the breeze had tugged one strand loose to dance it around one cheek. He saw how the smile had left her lips, but hadn't quite fled from her eyes.

Yeah, tasting wine with Chloe Merlin didn't seem like a bad way to spend an afternoon at all.

# Four

Since she began working as a personal chef five years earlier, Chloe had lived in some seriously beautiful homes, from her first job cooking for Lourdes and Alejandro Chavez in their charming Tribeca brownstone to Jack and Martin Ionesco's Fifth Avenue mansion a few years later to Anabel Carlisle's Park Avenue penthouse just weeks ago. All had been breathtaking in their own ways, and all of her employers had generously made clear she had the run of their homes in her off-time, be it their dens or their balconies or—in the case of the Ionescos— their home cinema. Hogan, too, had assured her she was welcome in any part of his house at any time.

But Chloe had never ventured out of her room in

any of her previous postings unless it was to cook in her employers' kitchens or to explore the culinary aspects of their various neighborhoods. She'd always been perfectly content to stay in her room reading books, watching movies or searching the internet for articles—but always something about cooking. She'd just never had the desire to involve herself any further in the homes or lives of her employers beyond cooking for them.

So why did she feel so restless in her room at Hogan's house? she wondered a few nights after their excursion to the wine-tasting—which had ended up being surprisingly enjoyable. And not just because Hogan had been such an agreeable companion, either. He'd also proved to have a fairly sophisticated palate, something that had astonished him as much as it had Chloe, and he had discovered some wines he actually enjoyed, all of them labels she would have chosen for him. She would have put his until then unknown oenophilia down to his Amherst genes, but somehow she suspected that whatever made Hogan Hogan was the result of Hogan alone. In any event, Chloe had actually almost had fun that day. She couldn't remember the last time she'd almost had fun.

Which was maybe why she suddenly felt so restless in her room. A part of her was itching to get out and almost have fun again. And no matter how sternly she told that part of herself to stop feeling that way, that part of herself refused to listen.

She looked at the clock on the nightstand. It was nearly midnight. Hogan, she knew, always turned in before eleven. She knew this because she often went to the kitchen to make a cup of *Mariage Frères* tea about that time before turning in herself, and the house was always locked up tight—dark and silent save a small lamp in the kitchen she required be kept on so that she could make late-night forages for things like *Mariage Frères* tea. She was confident enough he was in his own room by now that she didn't worry about having already donned her pajamas. Or what passed for pajamas for her—a pair of plaid flannel pajama pants and a T-shirt for François and the Atlas Mountains, her latest favorite band.

Even so, she padded as silently as she could in her sock feet down the stairs to the third floor—slowing only long enough at the fourth to ensure that, yes, Hogan's bedroom door was closed, and all the lights were off—where there was a library teeming with books, even though she was fairly sure they would be about things besides cooking. There might be a novel or two in the mix somewhere, and that would be acceptable.

The only light in the library was what spilled through the trio of arched floor-to-ceiling windows from a streetlamp outside—enough to tell her where the largest pieces of furniture lay, but not enough to distinguish any titles on book spines. So she switched on the first lamp she found, bathing the room in a pale, buttery glow.

She went to the set of shelves nearest her, pushing her glasses up on her nose so she could read the books' spines. All the titles there seemed to have something to do with maritime history. The next grouping was mostly atlases. After that came biographies, predominantly featuring robber barons, autocrats and politicians. So much for fun.

She went to the other side of the room and began working her way backward. Toward the middle, she finally came across novels. Lots of them. To her surprise, she found a number of historicals by Anya Seton, whom her grandmother had adored. She plucked out a title from the mix she recognized as one of Mémée's favorites, opened it to the first page, read a few lines and was immediately hooked. So hooked that she didn't look where she was going when she turned around and stepped away from the shelf, so she inadvertently toppled a floor lamp.

It fell to the ground, hitting the marble with what seemed like a deafening crash in the otherwise silent room. Hastily, she stooped to right it. No harm done, she decided when it was upright again with its shade back in place. Just to make sure, she flicked it on to see if the bulb still worked—it did—then turned it off again. After that the room—and the house—were silent once more.

She opened the book and went back to her reading, making her way slowly across the library as she did, skirting the furniture until she arrived back at the lamp she had turned on when she first entered. She stood there and continued to read until she finished a few more paragraphs, then absently turned off the light, closed the book and began picking her way through the darkness toward the wide library entrance—which, since she wasn't yet accustomed to the darkness, she had to struggle to make out, so her steps slowed even more. The moment she made her way through it and into the adjoining study, however, someone surged up behind her, wrapping an iron-hard arm around her waist to pull her back against himself—hard.

Chloe screamed at the top of her lungs and, simultaneously, elbowed him viciously in the gut and stomped down as hard as she could on his foot. When his grip on her loosened in response, she lurched away from him so fiercely that her glasses fell from her face and onto the floor. She barely noticed, though, because all of her attention went to hurling the heavy hardback as viciously as she could in the direction of her assailant—and hitting him square in the face with it if the expletive he yelled in response was any indication.

She was opening her mouth to scream again and about to race for the stairs when her attacker cried out, "Whoa, Chloe! I'm sorry! I didn't know it was you!"

Immediately, she closed her mouth. Hogan. Of course it was Hogan. Who else would it be? The house, she'd learned her first day on the job, had more security than Fort Knox, something she and Hogan both appeared to have forgotten. Realizing that now, however, did little to halt the flow of adrenaline to every cell in her body. Her heart was hammering, her breathing was ragged, her thoughts were scrambled and her body was trembling all over.

"I thought you were an intruder," he said.

He, too, sounded more than a little rattled—she could hear him breathing as heavily as she was. But his eyes must have been better adjusted to the dark, because he made his way effortlessly across the study to switch on a desktop lamp that threw the room into the same kind of soft, golden light the library had enjoyed only moments ago. In fact, the study was pretty much a smaller version of the room she'd just left.

Hogan, too, was bathed in soft, golden light, something that made him seem softer and more golden himself. His nightwear wasn't much different from hers, except that he was wearing sweatpants, and his T-shirt read "Vinnie's House of Hubcaps." And where her shirt hung loosely on her frame, Hogan's was stretched taut across his, so that it hugged every bump and groove of muscle and sinew on his torso. And there was a lot of muscle and sinew on his torso. And on his arms, too. Holy cow. His shirt-

sleeves strained against salient biceps that tapered
into a camber of muscles in his forearms in a way
that made her mouth go dry.

The moment Chloe realized she was staring, she
drove her gaze back up to his face. But that didn't
help at all, because his hair was adorably disheveled, his cheeks were shadowed by a day's growth
of beard and his bittersweet-chocolate eyes were
darker and more compelling than ever. Something
exploded in her belly and sent heat to every extremity, but not before much of it pooled deep in her
chest and womb.

Why did he have to be so handsome? So magnetic? So damnably sexy? And why couldn't she
ignore all of that? She encountered handsome, magnetic, sexy men all the time, and she never gave any
of them a second thought. What was it about Hogan
that made that impossible to do?

He was gripping a baseball bat about a third of the
way up, but he loosened his hold and let it slip to the
knob as he lowered it to his side. With his free hand,
he rubbed a spot on his forehead that was already
turning red—the place where the book had hit him.

"I am so sorry," she said. "I thought you were an
intruder, too."

He looked at his fingers, probably to check for
blood, and when he saw that they were clean, hooked
that hand on his hip. "Don't apologize for defending
yourself. It was a nice shot."

She tried to smile at that, but she was so rusty at smiling these days, she wasn't sure she succeeded. "Thanks."

"I heard a loud noise," he said. "I thought someone had broken in."

"That was me. I knocked over a lamp in the library. I came down to look for a book, and then I got so caught up in my reading that I didn't look where I was going. I didn't realize it was that loud. I mean, it sounded loud when it went down, but I thought that was just because the room was so quiet. I mean this house must have walls like a mausoleum, and—"

And she made herself shut up before she started to sound like an idiot, even though it was probably too late for that.

"No worries," he told her. "It's fine."

Oh, sure. Easy for him to say. He wasn't staring at some luscious blond wondering what he looked like under that T-shirt. And those sweatpants. And socks. And anything else he might be wearing. Or not wearing.

Oh, she really wished she hadn't thought that.

They stood there for another moment in silence, their gazes locked, their breathing still a little broken. Though hers was doubtless more a result of her thoughts than any lingering fear for her safety. Her physical safety anyway. Her mental and emotional safety were another matter at the moment.

Finally, Hogan said, "I think I need a drink." One

more look at her, and he added, "You look like you could use one, too."

She told herself to say no. Then said, "I wouldn't say no."

He nodded once, leaned the bat against a wide, heavy desk then crossed to a cabinet on the opposite side of the study, opening it to reveal a fairly substantial bar. Without even having to look through the options, he pulled down a bottle of very nice bourbon, along with a cut-crystal tumbler—obviously, he'd spent some time in this room—then turned around to look at Chloe.

"What's your poison?" he asked. "This is all bourbon. Something else my grandfather collected, I've discovered. If you'd rather have a glass of wine, I can go down to the cellar for some."

But she'd already recognized a familiar favorite on the shelf and shook her head. "I'll have a couple of fingers of the Angel's Envy," she told him.

His eyebrows shot up at that. "I never would have pegged you for a bourbon drinker."

"We're even, then," she said. "I wouldn't have guessed you'd be one, either." She'd been surprised enough at how quickly he'd taken to wine.

"I wasn't before," he admitted. "But after exploring my grandfather's study and discovering the bar, I realized cars weren't his only passion. I wanted to see if maybe we had this—" he gestured toward the spirits behind him "—in common, too." He grinned. "Turns out we do."

He withdrew her chosen label and a second tumbler for her and splashed a generous portion from each bottle into their respective glasses. Then he made his way back to her and handed her her drink, which she accepted gratefully.

He lifted his glass in a toast. "Here's to nonexistent intruders."

She lifted hers in response. "I'll drink to that."

They clinked their glasses and did so with enthusiasm, but after one taste, both seemed to lose track of where the conversation should go next. Chloe tried to focus on the heat of the bourbon as it warmed her stomach, but the heat in Hogan's eyes kept distracting her. He was looking at her differently from what she was used to, as if he were seeing something in her face that wasn't there before.

She realized what that was when he said, "You're not wearing your glasses. Or any lipstick. You're cute in them, but without them..."

It was only his mention of her glasses that made her remember she'd lost them in the scuffle. She really didn't need them that badly—only for up-close work—and mostly wore them because they were another way to keep distance between herself and others.

"I lost them when you, uh...when you, um..." *When you pulled me back against your rock-hard abs and made me want to crawl under your shirt to see them for myself* was the thought that tumbled through her mind, but she was pretty sure it wasn't a good idea to say that out loud. Especially since, at the time, what she'd really been thinking was that she needed to run for her life.

Then again, maybe the two thoughts had something in common after all.

He must have realized what she was trying to say—and thankfully not what she was actually thinking—because he glanced over toward the door where the two of them had been embraced a few minutes ago. Uh, she meant *embattled*, not *embraced*. Of course that was what she meant. Then he strode to the entryway, looked around on the floor and found them with little trouble. He picked up the book on his way back to Chloe and brought them both to her.

"Thanks," she said as she took her glasses from him. She started to put them back on then instead settled them on top of her head. She told herself it was only because she was sure they needed cleaning after what they'd just been through. It wasn't to get rid of any distance that might linger between Hogan and herself.

He looked at the spine of the book before handing it to her, eyeing her thoughtfully when he saw the unmistakably romantic title.

"It was Mémée's favorite," she said. Then, when

she realized he would have no idea who Mémée was, clarified, "My grandmother. Anya Seton was her favorite author, and when I saw all the books in the library by her, it made me think of Mémée, and I just—"

She'd just felt kind of lonely, she remembered, when she saw all the books that reminded her of the grandmother who passed away when she was in college. She thought about Mémée often—nearly every time she cooked—but somehow, seeing all those novels had roused feelings Chloe hadn't felt for a very long time. Or maybe it was something else that had done that. Since coming to work for Hogan, nothing in her life had felt normal.

"I thought reading it might make me feel closer to her," she said halfheartedly. Then, because she couldn't quite stop herself, she added, "I just miss her."

Hogan nodded. "I lost my folks young, too," he said. "How old were you when your grandmother died?"

"Nineteen."

"Which means you were even younger when you lost your parents."

"I never actually knew my parents," Chloe said, again without thinking. Wondering why she offered the information to Hogan when it was something she never discussed with anyone. She really must be frazzled by the whole intruder thing. Because even though she told her brain to stop talking, her mouth just kept it up. "My father was never in the picture—I'm not even sure my mother knew who he was—and not long after my mother had me, she sort of…disappeared."

Which was something Chloe *really* never talked about. Only one other person besides her grandmother knew about her origins. And that person was gone, too. What was possessing her to say all this to Hogan?

Whatever it was, it had such a hold on her that she continued, "My mother was troubled. Mémée did her best, but you can only do so much for a person who refuses to get help."

Hogan said nothing for a moment, then, softly, he told her, "I'm sorry." Probably because he didn't know what else to say. Not that Chloe blamed him. She wasn't sure what to say about her origins, either. Other than that they had made her what she was, so she couldn't—wouldn't—regret them.

"It's okay," she said. "Mémée was a wonderful parent. I had a nice childhood, thanks to her. I loved her very much, and she loved me."

Hogan gazed down into his drink. "So I guess you and I have something in common with the biological mother, what-if-things-had-been-different, kind of stuff, huh?"

Chloe started to deny it, started to tell him that her own upbringing would have been virtually the same if her mother had been healthy, then realized there was no way she could know that was true. Maybe her upbringing would have been better, maybe not. Who knew? But her mother would have been the one to mold her, not Mémée, and there was no way of even speculating about what shape Chloe would have taken. Would she have ever discovered her love of cooking under her mother's care? Or would she be passionate about something else now? Had her childhood been different, she might never have come to New York. She might never have met Hogan. Or anyone else.

"Maybe," she finally said. "But things happen to people every day that change their lives, many of them events that are out of their hands. Or by the smallest choices they make. Even opting to cross the street in one place instead of another could have devastating results if you get hit by a bus."

He smiled at that. "Yeah, well, I was thinking more in terms of our quality of life."

"You don't think you had quality of life growing up in Queens?"

"I had great quality of life growing up in Queens. The best. I'm kind of getting the impression that growing up here with the Amhersts would have left me at a disadvantage."

His response puzzled her. "Growing up in a breathtaking, multimillion-dollar home with unlimited funds at your disposal would have left you at a disadvantage?"

This time he nodded. "Sure. If no one here loved me."

Her heart turned over at the matter-of-fact way he said it. As if it was a given that he wouldn't have been loved here in this world of excess.

"You don't think your mother would have loved you?" she asked.

He expelled an errant breath and moved to sit in one of the leather chairs. Chloe followed, seating herself in the one next to it. She wasn't sure why—she really should be going back to her room and making the effort to get into bed—but something in his demeanor prohibited her from abandoning him just yet.

"I don't know," he said. "She was awfully young when she had me. She might have started looking at me as a liability who kept her from living the kind of life her friends did. She might have started resenting me. But I know my grandfather wouldn't have cared for me. His letter to me was—" he inhaled deeply and released the breath slowly "—not the warmest thing in the world. I mean, he wasn't mean or any-thing, but it was pretty clear he was only leaving his estate to me because the Amhersts dating all the way back to the time of knights and castles considered bloodline to be more important than anything else. He obviously wasn't happy about doing it."

He looked at something above the door. Chloe followed his gaze and saw an ornate coat of arms hanging there.

"The Amherst crest," he said. "There's one of those hanging in nearly every room in this house. Have you noticed?"

In truth, she hadn't. But when it came to physical surroundings, Chloe deliberately wasn't the most observant person in the world.

"No," she told him. "I suppose if there are that many, then bloodlines did indeed mean a lot to him."

"In his letter, he even asked that I consider legally changing my last name to Amherst so the direct line to the family name wouldn't die out with him. I guess he always figured Susan would forget about me and go on with her life. Get married and have other kids whose names she could hyphenate or something. Kids he could proudly call his progeny. His legacy. Instead of some grease monkey whose blue collar was stained with sweat."

"I'm sure Susan never forgot you, Hogan," Chloe said with absolute conviction. "And I'm sure she loved you very much. In a way, you were probably her first love. No one ever forgets or stops loving their first love."

He gave her another one of those thoughtful looks, the kind where the workings of his brain fairly shone in his eyes. His dark, beautiful, expressive eyes. "You sound like you're talking from experience."

She said nothing in response to that. She'd said too much already.

But her response must have shown on her face, too, because Hogan grinned a melancholy grin. "So there's some guy back there in your past you're still pining for, huh? The same way I've been pining for Anabel all these years? Is that something else you and I have in common?"

Maybe it was the bourbon. Maybe it was the pale, otherworldly light. Maybe it was the last lingering traces of mind-scrambling adrenaline. Maybe it was just the way Hogan was looking at her. Whatever it was, Chloe couldn't resist it.

"I'm not pining for him," she said. "I'll never get him back. He's gone."

Hogan's grin fell. He met her gaze levelly, and whatever he saw in her eyes made his eyebrows arrow downward and his jaw clench tight. "Gone," he repeated. "Gone like…he moved to another country?"

Chloe shook her head. It wasn't the bourbon. It wasn't the light. It wasn't the adrenaline. It was definitely Hogan this time and the way he was looking at her that made her say the rest.

"Samuel was my husband. He was a chef, too. We were going to open our own restaurant. We were going to have kids and teach them to cook, too. We were going to have a long life together, full of family and food. We were going to retire fat and happy in Lyon, and we were going to have our ashes scattered together in the Pyrenees. Instead, his ashes were scattered in Brown County State Park, where he and I had our first date when we were in ninth grade."

Hogan was looking kind of horrified now, confirming what Chloe already suspected—she had made her biggest mess yet. So she gripped her glass and downed what was left of its contents. Then she rose and carried it back to the cabinet from which Hogan had taken it. She started to leave it there for him to take to the kitchen with his own glass when he was ready. Instead, she picked up the bottle of bourbon that was still sitting on the bar and left with both it and the glass. It was definitely time to go back to her room and make the effort to get into bed. Somehow, though, she knew it was going to be a while before she actually made it to sleep.

# Five

Hogan didn't expect to see Chloe the morning after she bared the depths of her soul to him. Not just because a person as private as she was would obviously be embarrassed about having revealed what she had last night, but because he knew firsthand what too much bourbon—even good bourbon—could do to a person. She'd looked pretty serious about making a dent in the bottle she'd taken back to her room.

So it surprised him when he went into the kitchen Friday morning to make himself breakfast and found her in there cooking. She was wearing one of her gigantic chef's jackets and gaudy pants—these decorated with silhouettes of pigs and the word "oink"—and had her hair gathered at the top of her head the way she always did. Her glasses were back in place, her red lipstick was perfect and she looked none the worse for wear for having been up late drinking and grieving for a man she would have loved for the rest of her life if he hadn't died far too soon.

He still couldn't believe she was a widow at twenty-eight. Had been a widow since twenty-three or younger, considering she'd been in New York cooking for people for the past five years. Though her revelation last night went a long way toward explaining why she was the way she was, cool and aloof and serious to a fault. Had Hogan experienced what she had, had he, say, married Anabel and then lost her so young, he would have been putting his fist through something every chance he got. And there wouldn't have been enough bourbon in the world to keep him numb.

Then he remembered that Chloe wasn't cool or aloof or serious to a fault. There had been moments since he'd met her when her veneer had cracked enough for him to see through to the other side. That day in the gallery when she told him his feelings of confusion about his place in the world were valid. That afternoon of the wine-tasting when she uttered that erotic little sound at the touch of his thumb. Last night when she fought like a tiger for her safety. Chloe Merlin had a sensitive, passionate, fiery soul, one that clawed its way out of wherever she buried it whenever her guard was down. Though, now that he knew more about her, he understood her guardedness. He just wished she didn't feel like she had to be so wary around him.

"Good morning," he said as he headed for the coffeemaker.

She jumped at the sound of his voice and spun around, but her expression offered nothing of what she might be feeling.

"Your breakfast will be ready in ten minutes," she said in reply.

"Great," he told her. "But you know, after last night, you didn't have to—"

"Your breakfast will be ready in ten minutes," she repeated before he could finish, in exactly the same way.

"But—"

"Your breakfast will be ready in ten minutes," she said a third time, more adamantly. Then, to drive that point home, she added, "Have a seat in your dining room, and I'll bring it out to you."

Ah. Okay. So they were just going to ignore what happened last night and go back to the way things were. Pretend she never said all the things she said— and pretend he never saw her looking all soft and vulnerable and pretty.

Which should have been fine. They had separate lives that didn't need to intersect except for mealtimes or if he happened to run into her in the house at some point.

Like he had last night.

He guessed that was beside the point—Chloe's point anyway. And it was a good point. For some reason, though, Hogan didn't want to take it. He didn't want to forget last night happened. He didn't want to forget what she said. He didn't want to forget how she looked. And he didn't want to go back to their old routine and roles.

Chloe obviously did, though. So, without saying anything more, he poured himself a cup of coffee—ignoring her frown, since, as far as she was concerned, that was her job—then went to the dining room to wait for his breakfast.

But when he sat down at the table—the same way he'd sat down at the table every morning for a few weeks now—he didn't feel any more comfortable than he had on any of the other mornings waiting for his breakfast. Maybe a legal document had made this place his house, but it still didn't feel like home. Maybe he never had to work another day in his life, but his life right now didn't have any purpose. Maybe he was eating better than he ever had before, but he didn't like eating by the clock and by himself. Hell, at least he'd had the Mets and the Knicks to keep him company before.

Hogan's point was that he didn't like having someone else fixing and bringing him his break-

fast. Even if hiring Chloe to do just that had been—
and still was—the best way to bring Anabel back
into his life. Which was something he needed to be
focusing his attention on. And he would. ASAP. Just
as soon as he figured out a way to do it that would
keep Anabel in his house for longer than the few
minutes she'd been here last time.

For now, though, he'd just have to keep putting
up with breakfast Chloe's way instead of making
his own, the way he'd been doing from the time he
was a preschooler splashing more milk out of the
cereal bowl than into it all the way up to grabbing a
cruller from Alpha Donuts on his way to work. That
was breakfast for normal people. Breakfast wasn't—

Chloe arrived at his side and set a plate in front of
him. Beside a couple of slices of melon settled into
what he'd come to recognize as chard was a wedge
of something layered with… Ah, hell. He was too
tired to try to identify what all the layers were.

So he asked, "What's that?"

"*Tartiflette avec les lardons, le reblochon et les
truffes noires.*"

"Which is?"

"Potato casserole with bacon, cheese and mushrooms."

Hogan sighed. Breakfast wasn't *tarti*-whatever.
It wasn't even potato casserole with bacon, cheese
and mushrooms. He started to tell Chloe he'd have
breakfast out this morning. He could take the train

to Queens and stop by Alpha Donuts to treat himself to a baker's dozen. He could visit the garage while he was in the neighborhood, maybe go back to his old apartment for a few things he hadn't thought he'd need here. And then he could grab lunch at Taco Taberna across the street before he came ho— Before he came back to Lenox Hill.

He glanced at Chloe. Up close, she didn't look as put together as he first thought. In fact, up close, he could see smudges of purple beneath red-rimmed eyes and a minuscule smudge of lipstick at the corner of her usually flawlessly painted mouth. Not to mention an expression on her face that was a clear mix of *I'm-the-fiercest-human-being-in-the-world* and *I'm-barely-holding-it-together.* She'd gotten up early on a morning when she probably felt like crap because she had to do her job. She'd dressed and hauled herself into work, even though she probably felt uncomfortable facing her boss. Hogan would be the biggest mook in New York if he left now.

"It looks delicious," he told her. "Thank you."

She looked surprised by his gratitude. This after he'd thanked her every time she brought him a meal. But she replied, as she always did, "You're welcome." Then she spun on her heel to return to the kitchen.

As he often did, Hogan turned around to watch her retreat. Usually, she headed straight for her sanctuary, head held high, her step never faltering. This morning, though, she moved sluggishly, her head dipping down. She even lifted her hand to her face at one point, and he was pretty sure she was wiping something out of her eyes.

He turned back around and looked at his breakfast. Even if it wasn't what he usually ate, it was, like everything else she'd cooked, very…artful. In fact, it was, like everything else she'd cooked, almost too artful to eat.

He suddenly wondered what chefs fed themselves. Did Chloe prepare her own breakfast as painstakingly as she made his? Or was she in the kitchen right now, jamming a Pop-Tart into her mouth without even bothering to toast it first? Would her lunch be a slice of reheated pizza? With maybe some Sara Lee pound cake for dessert? Hogan really liked Sara Lee pound cake. He missed Sara Lee pound cake. And, while he was at it, when did Chloe eat dinner anyway? Before or after she made his? Did she fix a double batch of everything? One for him and one for her? Or did she just throw together a ham and cheese sandwich to eat while she was waiting for him to finish? A real ham and cheese sandwich. Not a French one.

He was still wondering about all that as he picked up his fork and dug in to the potato whatever. And he wondered about something else, too: How did he convince his chef there was more to life than timetables and fancy potato casseroles?

* * *

By the time Chloe left for her grocery shopping Friday afternoon, she felt almost human again. A midmorning nap—which she took completely by accident in Hogan's wine cellar when she lay down to look at the bottles on the very bottom shelf—had helped. What helped more was Hogan's acceptance that they pretend last night never happened. But what helped most of all was losing herself in the sounds and sights and smells of Greenmarket, scouring the farmers' stalls for what seasonal finds this early November day had to offer. She needed shallots for the *confit de canard* she would be making for dinner, Brussels sprouts and mesclun to go with, and pears for the *clafoutis* she planned for dessert.

She took her time as she wandered through the market, stopping at a stall whenever she saw a particularly delectable-looking piece of produce to wonder what she could make with it. The apples always smelled so luscious this time of year. And there was a vendor with maple syrup. Had to have some of that. Oh, and fennel! She hadn't made anything with fennel for a long time. Fennel was delicious in vichyssoise. Had to have some of that, too. And this would be the last of the tomatoes until next year. She should probably pick up a few and use them for something, too. Maybe a nice *tartine*…

By the time Chloe returned from Greenmarket, she had two canvas totes teeming with vegetables and fruits and other goodies, more than enough to get her through Friday and Saturday both. Enough, really, so that Hogan could have leftovers on Sunday if he wanted to fix something for himself while she was out doing something. Something that wasn't staying in Hogan's house. Something that kept her mind busy with thoughts that had nothing to do with Hogan. Or the way Hogan looked last night after she told him about Samuel. Or thoughts about Samuel, for that matter. Or anything other than food and its preparation. Its wonderful, methodical, intricate preparation that could keep even the most prone-to-wandering-to-places-it-really-shouldn't-wander mind focused on the task at hand.

She couldn't wait to get started on dinner.

She had just finished putting everything away—save what she would be using tonight—and was about to head to her room to change from her khaki cargo pants and baggy pomegranate-colored sweater into her chef's duds, when Hogan entered the kitchen carrying two white plastic bags decorated with the red logo of a local grocery chain.

"I'm cooking tonight," he said without preamble when he saw her. Before she could object, he hurried on, "I was in my old neighborhood today to stop by my old place, and I dropped in at the market where I used to shop, and—"

"Why did you have to go to the market there?" Chloe interrupted.

She didn't mean to be rude. She was just so surprised and flustered by his appearance in the kitchen again—save this morning, he hadn't ventured into the room once since that first day when he greeted her here—that she didn't know what else to say. And that could also be the only explanation for why she sounded not just rude, but also a tad jealous, when she said what she did.

Hogan must have heard the accusatory tone in her voice, too, because he suddenly looked a little guilty. All he said, though, was, "I needed a few things."

"What kind of things?"

His guilty look compounded. "Uh…things. You know. Personal things. Things I needed to get. That are personal."

"And you had to go all the way to Queens? Does Manhattan not have these personal things you needed?"

And could she just stop talking? Chloe demanded of herself. She sounded like a suspicious wife. Where Hogan went, what he bought, why he went there and bought it was none of her business. *For God's sake, shut* up, *Chloe.*

"Sure, I could have gotten them here," he said. "But C-Town is right up the street from the garage, and it was on the way to the train, so I went in there. For some things. And while I was there, I picked up some stuff for dinner. I thought I could give you a break."

*A break?* she echoed incredulously to herself. She hadn't even been working for him for a month, and already he was tired of her cooking? No one got tired of Chloe's cooking. Not only was it the best in New York, they also paid her too much to get tired of her cooking.

"Dinner is my job," she reminded him. "It's what you pay me to do. I don't need a break."

"I know, but I thought—"

"Am I not performing to your standards?" she asked.

Now he looked surprised. "What? Of course you are. I just—"

"Have I not cooked you acceptable meals?"

"Yes, Chloe, everything you've cooked has been great, but—"

"Then why do you suddenly want to cook for yourself?"

And why did she still sound like a possessive spouse? Bad enough she was grilling him about things she had no business grilling him about. She was only making it worse sounding like she thought she was entitled to do it. Even if she did have some bizarre desire to actually be Hogan's spouse—which she of course did *not*—it was Anabel Carlisle he wanted to cast in that role. Chloe was his *chef.* So why wasn't she acting like one?

Hogan didn't seem to be offended by her outburst, though. In fact, he suddenly looked kind of relieved.

He even smiled. "No, Chloe, you don't understand. I'm not cooking for myself. I'm cooking for us."

Okay, now she was really confused. As weird as it was for her to be behaving like a scorned lover, it was even weirder for Hogan to be acting like a cheerful suitor. Especially one who could cook.

Before she could say anything else, though, he was emptying the contents of the bags onto the kitchen island. A pound of ground chuck, a couple of white onions, a bag of shredded, store brand "Mexican blend" cheese, a bag of tortilla chips and a jar of salsa—both of those were store brand, too—a packet of mass-produced taco seasoning, a bottle of mass-produced taco sauce and a half dozen generic white eggs.

She hastily added up the ingredients in her chef's brain and blanched when she calculated the sum. "Oh, my God. You're going to make taco meatloaf, aren't you?"

He was fairly beaming as he withdrew a burned and battered loaf pan.

"Yep," he said proudly. "In the sacred Dempsey meatloaf pan, which is the mother of all meatloaf pans. On account of it was my mother's. And it gets even better."

He spoke as if that were a paean.

What he withdrew from the second sack was a bag of frozen "crinkle cut" carrots, which he said would be divine with a glaze of butter and Sucanat—

except he really said they would taste great stirred up in a pan with some margarine and brown sugar, both of which he was sure Chloe had on hand—then came a tube of prefab biscuits whose label proudly proclaimed, "With flaky layers!" And then—*then*— to her absolute horror, he withdrew the single most offensive affront to gastronomy any chef could possibly conceive: a box of—Chloe could scarcely believe her eyes—macaroni and cheese.

"But wait, that's still not the best part," he told her.

Well, of course it wasn't the best part. There was no *best part* of anything sitting on the counter. He could pull a rabid badger out of the bag, and it would still be better than anything he'd removed so far. But it wasn't a rabid badger he pulled out of the bag. It was far, far worse. A ready-made pound cake wrapped in tinfoil that looked dense enough to, if there were a few thousand more of them, build a garage, followed by a gigantic plastic tub of something called Fros-Tee Whip, which self-identified as a "non-dairy whipped topping." Chloe couldn't help but recoil.

"I know, right?" Hogan said, evidently mistaking her flinch of repugnance for a tremor of excitement. "It's the greatest dessert ever invented by humankind."

This was going to be news to the creators of *crème brûlée, crêpes Suzette* and *soufflé au chocolat*.

"Look, I know you're not big on the processed foods," he said when he saw her looking at the assortment of, um, groceries. "But you're going to love all this. And I got the good kind of mac and cheese. The kind with the liquid cheese in the pouch, not the powdered stuff in the envelope."

Oh, well, in *that* case...

When she looked at him again, he was grinning in a way that let her know he was perfectly aware that the meal he was proposing was the complete antithesis of epicurean. But he clearly intended to prepare it anyway.

"Hogan, do you realize how much sodium there is in that pile of...of...?" she asked.

"I think 'food products' is the phrase you're looking for," he supplied helpfully.

Actually, she had been thinking of another word entirely. Even so, the *products* part of his suggestion, she would concede. It was the *food* part she found debatable. So she only reiterated, "Hogan, do you realize how much sodium there is in that pile?"

He grinned. "Chloe, I don't care how much sodium there is in that pile. No one cares how much sodium comes out of their grocery bags."

"People who want to live to see their first gray hair do."

"This—" he pointed at his purchases on the island "—is a lot closer to the typical American diet than that is." Now he pointed at the items from her shopping trip she'd left on the counter. "Not to mention the typical American diet is a lot easier to prepare."

"Ease does not equate to edible. Or enjoyable."

"It does when it's taco meatloaf."

"If this—" now Chloe was the one to point to the…groceries…he'd bought "—is the sort of thing you want to eat, then why did you hire me to cook for you in the first place?"

She knew the answer to that question, of course. He was using her to get Anabel Carlisle's attention. Chloe knew that because Hogan himself had said so and, hey, it hadn't made any difference to her. It was irrelevant. She worked for whoever paid her the most. That was rule number one when it came to choosing her employers. For some reason, though, it suddenly kind of bothered her to be used as a means to an end. Especially that end in particular.

Hogan's reply, however, had nothing to do with Anabel. In fact, it wasn't a reply at all. At least not to the question she'd asked.

"Come on. Let me cook dinner tonight," he cajoled. "Have you ever even eaten taco meatloaf?"

She gave him one of those *What do you think?* looks and said nothing.

"Then how do you know you won't like it?" he asked.

"Two words. Butylated hydroxyanisole."

*"Gesundheit."* He grinned again.

And damn that grin anyway, because every time she saw it, something in Chloe's chest grew warmer.

At this point, it was also spreading into body parts that really shouldn't be feeling warm in mixed company.

"I guarantee you'll love it," he told her. "If you don't, I promise I'll never invade your kitchen again."

She started to remind him that the room they were standing in was actually *his* kitchen, but hesitated. For some reason she did feel a little proprietary when it came to Hogan's kitchen. Certainly more than she had any other kitchen where she'd worked. She told herself it was because it was less sterile than most with its tile the color of the French Riviera and its creamy enamel appliances and its gleaming copper pots that dangled like amaranth from the ceiling and its gigantic windows that spilled more sunshine in one morning than she'd seen working for months in most places. From the moment she'd set foot in here, she'd coveted this kitchen. In the weeks that followed, she'd come to feel as if she never wanted to leave.

Though, if she were honest with herself, there were days, she supposed, when she wasn't sure that was entirely because of the kitchen.

"Fine," she conceded reluctantly. "You can cook dinner tonight."

"For us," he clarified.

Although she wasn't sure why he needed or wanted that concession—and although she wasn't sure it was a good idea for her to make it—Chloe echoed, "For us."

* * *

When Hogan had gotten the bright idea to cook taco meatloaf for Chloe, he'd been wanting something for dinner that was a taste of home—his real home, not his adopted one. He'd been lying under the chassis of a Dodge Charger at the time—one Eddie Deflorio was thinking of buying, to give it a once-over and make sure Eddie wasn't about to get shafted—when Eddie said something about Hogan's mom's taco meatloaf. And just like that, Hogan had been jonesing for it more than he had in years. And not just the taco meatloaf, but also the carrots and biscuits and mac and cheese his mom always made to go with it. And—it went without saying—some Sara Lee pound cake for dessert.

It had just felt so good to be back in the garage, surrounded by familiar sounds and smells and people, talking about familiar stuff—not to mention *doing* something—that Hogan had just wanted the day to go on for as long as it could. And he'd wanted to keep *doing* something. Even if it was making taco meatloaf. If he was going to do that, then he had to go up to his old apartment to get his mom's meatloaf pan. Then, once he was back in his apartment…

He'd just felt better than he had in weeks. He'd felt like he was home. Then he'd realized he wanted to share that feeling with someone. And the person that popped into his head was Chloe Merlin. She had shared something of herself with him last night and obviously wished she hadn't. Now he wanted to share something with her so she wouldn't feel like she had to hide her emotions. From him or anyone else.

What better way to share a piece of his neighborhood home with her than to bring a taste of Queens into a kitchen of Lenox Hill?

Thankfully, Chloe had hung around while he was putting together the meatloaf to tell him where everything was, even if he sometimes had to walk clear across the room to find what he needed. Mostly, she had sat on a stool sipping a glass of red wine, throwing out words like *monosodium glutamate* and *propyl gallate* and *potassium bromate*. But she'd at least poured him a glass of wine, too, and turned on some halfway decent music to cook by, even if he didn't understand a word of what was being sung.

He had managed to combine all the ingredients of the dish and make a fairly serviceable loaf out of it—even if it was a little bigger on one end than the other, something that, now that he thought about it, actually made it more authentic—and was ready to put in the oven, when he realized he forgot to turn on the oven to preheat it. Which, now that he thought about that, too, also made the experience more authentic. What didn't make it authentic was that he had no idea how to work the damned stove, because it was three times the size of a normal stove and had roughly a billion knobs on it.

"How do you turn this thing on?" he asked Chloe.

She had finally ended her indictment of the processed food industry and was now reading a book about somebody named Auguste Escoffier—in French. She looked up at the question, studying Hogan over the tops of her glasses for a moment. Then she pushed them into place with the back of her hand, set her book down on the counter and rose to cross to the stove.

"What temperature do you need?" she asked.

"Three-fifty," he told her.

She flipped one of the knobs, and the oven emitted a soft, satisfying hiss. "Give it a minute."

She looked at the meatloaf, still sitting on the kitchen island in its pan, surrounded by stray bits of onion and cheese, splatters of salsa and a fine dusting of taco seasoning. Okay, and also a little puddle of wine, the result of Hogan having an accident during a momentary wild idea to add some red wine to the meatloaf, thinking maybe that would make Chloe like it better. Fortunately, he came to his senses before doing it, mostly to keep his mother from spinning in her grave, but also because he wasn't sure he was ready to wing it in the kitchen just yet. Chloe looked back at him, took off her glasses and met his gaze levelly. *"Ce travail, c'est pas de la tarte, n'est-ce pas?"*

He had no idea what she said, but he was pretty sure by her expression that she was commiserating with him. He was also pretty sure that the reason he was suddenly getting kind of aroused was because she just spoke French. And call him crazy, but arousal probably wasn't a good idea in the middle of a kitchen when the meatloaf wasn't even in the oven yet. Which was *not* a euphemism for *any*thing sexual.

"Uh…" he began eloquently.

She emitted a soft sigh, folded her glasses and set them on the counter, then gave him another one of those almost-smiles he'd seen from her once or twice. And liked. A lot.

"Cooking isn't for the fainthearted," she told him. "It's harder than people think."

Yeah, and he was only using like five ingredients, most of which came out of boxes and bags. He couldn't imagine how much trouble Chloe went to whenever she prepared a meal.

"Thanks for your help," he said.

"I didn't do anything."

"You told me where to find the scissors. That was major."

She almost smiled again.

"And you poured me a glass of wine. That was really major."

"It was the least I could do."

"Thanks again."

They stood staring at each other for another minute, Hogan trying not to notice how beautiful her green eyes were, or how great she looked wearing something besides her giant chef clothes, or how her hair was longer than he first thought, falling past her shoulders in a rush of near-white silk. Those weren't things he should be noticing about his chef. They were things he should be noticing about Anabel. Things he doubtless *would* notice about Anabel, once the two of them got together again. Just as soon as he called her up and invited her to, um, do something. Which he would totally figure out. Soon.

"The stove is ready," Chloe said.

Stove? he wondered. What stove? Oh, right. The one they were standing right next to. That must be the reason he was suddenly feeling so hot.

"Isn't there a beeper or something that's supposed to go off to tell us that?" he asked.

She shook her head. And kept looking at him as intently as he was looking at her. "Not on a stove like this."

"Then how do you know it's ready?"

"I just know."

Of course she did.

"So I guess I should put the meatloaf in the oven, then," he said. Not thinking about any kind of sexual euphemisms *at all*.

"I guess you should."

Hogan nodded. Chloe nodded. But neither of them did anything. Finally, she took the initiative and picked up the pan. Then she opened the oven and pushed in the meatloaf. Really deep. Pretty much as far as it would go. Hogan tried not to notice. He did. Honest.

"There," she said, straightening as she closed the oven door. "How long does it need to go?"

Oh, it needed to go for a very long time, he wanted to say. Hours and hours and hours. Maybe all night. What he said, though, was, "Sixty minutes ought to do it."

Chloe nodded. Hogan nodded. And he wondered how the hell he ever could have thought it would be a good idea to cook dinner for Chloe in a hot kitchen with an even hotter oven.

"I should probably clean up my mess," he said.

But there weren't enough cleaners in the world to take care of the mess he'd made today. He was supposed to be focused on winning back Anabel. But lately, he was hardly ever even thinking about Anabel. Because, lately, his head was too full of Chloe.

Yeah, Chloe. A woman who had pledged her life to a man she'd lost much too young. And who was still grieving for him five years later. And who would probably never want anyone else again.

# Six

"So? Come on. What did you think?"

Chloe looked at Hogan from her seat on his right at his gigantic dinner table. He was beaming like a kid who'd just presented for show-and-tell a salamander he fished out of the creek all by himself.

"You liked it, didn't you?" he asked. "I can tell, because you cleaned your plate. Welcome to the clean plate club, Chloe Merlin."

"It was…acceptable," she conceded reluctantly.

He chuckled. "Acceptable. Right. You had second helpings of everything, and you still cleaned your plate."

"I just wanted to be sure I ate enough for an accurate barometer of the taste combinations, that's all."

"And the taste combinations were really good, weren't they?"

All right, fine. Taco meatloaf had a certain *je ne sais quoi* that was surprisingly appealing. So did the carrots. And even the biscuits. Chloe had never eaten anything like them in her life. Mémée had never allowed anything frozen or processed in the house when Chloe was growing up. Her grandmother had kept a small greenhouse and vegetable garden in the backyard, and what she hadn't grown herself, she'd bought at the weekly visits she and Chloe made to the farmers' markets or, in the coldest months, at the supermarket—but organic only.

Chloe had just never felt the urge to succumb to the temptation of processed food, even if it was more convenient. She *enjoyed* prepping and cooking meals. She *enjoyed* buying the ingredients fresh. The thought of scooping food out of bags and jars and boxes was as alien to her as having six limbs. It wasn't that she was a snob about food or cooking, it was just that…

Okay, she was kind of a snob about food and cooking. Clearly, her beliefs could use some tweaking.

"You know," she told Hogan, "I could make some taco seasoning myself for you to use next time, from my own spice collection. It would have a lot less sodium in it."

He grinned. "That would be great. Thanks."

"And salsa is easy to make. I could make some of that fresh, the next time you want to cook this."

"I'd love that."

"Even the biscuits could be made—"

"I have to stop you there," he interjected. "I'm sorry, but the biscuits have to be that specific kind. They're what my mom always made. It's tradition."

And it was a taste of his childhood. Chloe got that. She felt the same way about *gratin Dauphinois*.

"Okay," she conceded. "But maybe fresh carrots next time, instead of frozen?"

He thought about that for a minute. "Okay. I mean, we already changed those anyway, since that stuff you call brown sugar is actually beige sugar, and you didn't have any margarine. By the way, what kind of person doesn't have margarine in their kitchen?"

Before, Chloe would have answered a question like that with some retort about hexane and free radicals. Instead, she said, "Butter is better for you."

She managed to stop herself before adding, *And you need to stay healthy, Hogan*. Because what she would have added after that was *I need you to be healthy, Hogan*.

She refused to think any further than that. Such as *why* she needed Hogan to be healthy. She told herself it was for the same reason she wanted any-one to be healthy. Everyone deserved to live a long, happy life. No one knew that better than Chloe, who

had seen one of the kindest, most decent human be-
ings she'd ever known have his life jerked out from
under him. She didn't want the same thing to happen to Hogan. Not that it would. The man looked as
hearty as a longshoreman. But Samuel had looked
perfectly healthy, too, the day he left for work in the
morning and never came home again.

She pushed the thought away and stood. "Since
you cooked, I'll clean up. It's only fair."

Hogan looked a little startled by her abrupt announcement, but stood, too. "You helped cook. I'll
help clean up."

She started to object but he was already picking
up his plate and loading it with his flatware. So she
did likewise and followed him to the kitchen. Together they loaded the dishwasher. Together they
packed the leftovers in containers. Together they
put them in the fridge.

And together they decided to open another bottle of wine.

But it was Hogan's suggestion that they take it
up to the roof garden. Although he'd told her on
her first day at work the house had one, and that
she should feel free to use it whenever she wanted,
especially since he probably never would, Chloe
hadn't yet made her way up there. She really did
prefer to stay in her room when she wasn't working
or out and about. Save that single excursion to the
library—and look how that had turned out. When

they made it up onto the roof, however, she began to think maybe she should reconsider. New York City was lovely at night.

So was Hogan's rooftop garden. The living section—which was nearly all of it—was a patchwork of wooden flooring and was lit by crisscrossing strings of tiny white lights woven through an overhead trellis. Terra-cotta pots lined the balustrade, filled with asters and camellias and chrysanthemums, all flaming with autumn colors from saffron to cinnamon to cayenne. Beyond it, Manhattan twinkled like tidy stacks of gemstones against the night sky.

Knowing the evening would be cool, Chloe had grabbed a wrap on her way up, a black wool shawl that had belonged to her grandmother, embroidered with tiny red flowers. She hugged it tightly to herself as she sat on a cushioned sofa pushed against a brick access bulkhead and set her wine on a table next to it. Hogan sat beside her, setting his wine on a table at his end. For a long moment neither spoke. They only gazed out at the glittering cityscape in silence.

Finally, Chloe said, "I still have trouble sometimes believing I live in New York. I kind of fell in love with the city when I was a kid, reading about it and seeing so many movies filmed here. I never actually thought I'd be living here. Especially in a neighborhood like this."

"Yeah, well, I grew up in New York," Hogan said,

"but this part of the city is as foreign to me as the top of the Himalayas would be. I still can't believe I live here, either. I never came into Manhattan when I was a kid. Especially someplace like Park Avenue. I never felt the need to."

"Then how did you meet Anabel?" Chloe asked. "She doesn't seem like the type to ever leave Park Avenue."

He grinned that damnably sexy grin again. He'd done that a lot tonight. And every time he did, Chloe felt a crack open in the armor she'd worn so well for so long, and a little chink of it tumbled away. At this point, there were bits of it strewn all over his house, every piece marking a place where Hogan had made her feel something after years of promising herself she would never feel anything again. What she ought to be feeling was invaded, overrun and offended. Instead, she felt…

Well. Things she had promised herself she would never feel again—had sworn she was incapable of ever feeling again. Things that might very well get her into trouble.

"How I met Anabel is actually kind of a funny story," Hogan said. "She and a couple of her friends were going to a concert at Shea Stadium, but they pissed off their cab driver so bad on the way, he stopped the car in the middle of the street in front of my dad's garage and made them get out. She and the guy got into a shouting match in the middle of

Jamaica Avenue, and a bunch of us working in the garage went out to watch." He chuckled. "I remember her standing there looking like a bohemian princess and cursing like a sailor, telling the cabbie she knew the mayor personally and would see to it that he never drove a cab in the tristate area again."

Chloe smiled at the picture. She couldn't imagine Anabel Carlisle, even a teenaged one, behaving that way. Her former employer had always been the perfect society wife when Chloe worked for her.

"Anyway, after the cabbie drove off without them, all us guys started applauding and whistling. Anabel spun around, and I thought she was going to give us a second helping of what she'd just dished out, but she looked at me and..." He shook his head. "I don't know. It was like how you see someone, and there's just something there. The next thing I knew, me and a couple of the guys are walking up the street with her and her friends, and we're all going for pancakes. After that she came into Queens pretty often. She even had dinner at my house with me and my folks a few times. But she never invited me home to meet hers."

There was no bitterness in his voice when he said that last sentence. There was simply a matter-of-factness that indicated he understood why she hadn't wanted to include him in her uptown life. That was gentlemanly of him, even if Chloe couldn't understand Anabel's behavior. She imagined Hogan had been just as nice back then as he was now. Anabel must have realized that if she'd become involved with him. Who cared what neighborhood he called home?

"It was her parents," he said, as if he'd read her mind. "Her dad especially didn't want her dating outside her social circle. She would have gotten into a lot of trouble if they found out about me. I understood why she couldn't let anyone know she was involved with me."

"If you understood," Chloe said, "then how come you're still unattached after all this time? Why have you waited for her?"

She thought maybe she'd overstepped the bounds—again—by asking him something so personal. But Hogan didn't seem to take offense.

"I didn't sit around for fifteen years waiting for her," he said. "I dated other girls. Other women. I just never met anyone who made me feel the way Anabel did, you know? There was never that spark of lightning with anyone else like there was that night on Jamaica Avenue."

Chloe didn't understand that, either. Love wasn't lightning. She did, however, understand seeing a person and just knowing there was something there. That had happened to her, too. With Samuel. The day he walked into English class in the middle of freshman year, she'd looked up from *The Catcher in the Rye* and into the sweetest blue eyes she'd ever seen, and she'd known at once that there was something between them. Something. Not love. Love came later. Because love was something so momentous, so stupendous, so enormous, that it had to happen over time. At least it did for Chloe. For Hogan, evidently, it took only a sudden jolt of electricity.

"And now Anabel is free," she said, nudging aside thoughts of the past in an effort to get back to the present. "You must feel as if you're being tasered within an inch of your life these days."

Even if he hadn't done much in the way of trying to regain the affections of his former love, she couldn't help thinking. She wondered why he hadn't.

He looked thoughtful for a moment. "I think maybe I've outgrown the fireworks part," he said cryptically. "But yeah. I really need to call her and set something up."

"Why don't you have a dinner party and invite her?" Chloe suggested. Wondering why her voice sounded so flat. She loved preparing meals for dinner parties. It was great fun putting together the menus. "You could ask her and a few other couples. Maybe she's still friends with some of the girls who were with her the night you met her," she added, trying to get into the spirit. And not getting into the spirit at all. "Other people would offer a nice buffer for the two of you to get reacquainted."

By the time she finished speaking, there was the oddest bitterness in Chloe's mouth. Maybe the wine had turned. Just to make sure, she took another sip. No, actually, the pinot noir tasted quite good.

"Maybe," Hogan said.

"No, definitely," she insisted. Because...

Well, just because. That was why. And it was an excellent reason. Hogan clearly needed a nudge in Anabel's direction, since he wasn't heading that way himself. He'd made clear since Chloe's first day of employment that he was still pining for the woman he'd loved since he was a teenager. He needed a dinner party. And Chloe needed a dinner party, too. Something to focus on that would keep her mind off things it shouldn't be on.

"Look, Chloe," he said, "I appreciate your wanting to help, but—"

"It will be perfect," she interrupted him. "Just a small party of, say, six or eight people."

"But—"

"I can get it all organized by next weekend, provided everyone is available."

"But—"

"Don't worry about a thing. I'll take care of all the details. It will be your perfect entrée into society, which, for some reason, you haven't made yet."

"Yeah, because—"

"A week from tomorrow. If you'll supply the names, I'll make the calls to invite everyone."

"Chloe—"

"Just leave it to me."

He opened his mouth to protest again, but seemed to have run out of objections. In fact, he kind of looked like the proverbial deer in the headlights. Okay, proverbial stag in the headlights.

Then he surprised her by totally changing the subject. "So what was it like growing up in... Where did you say you're from? Someplace in Indiana."

"New Albany," she replied automatically. "It's in the southern part of the state, on the Ohio River."

"I'm going to go out on a limb and say it probably wasn't much like Manhattan," he guessed. "Or even Queens."

"No, not at all. It's quiet. Kind of quirky. Nice. It was a good place to grow up." She couldn't quite stop herself from drifting back into memories again. "Not a whole lot to do when you're a kid, but still nice. And Louisville was right across the river, so if we wanted the urban experience, we could go over there. Not that it was as urban as here, of course. But there were nights when we were teenagers when Samuel and I would ride our bikes down to the river and stare at Louisville on the other side. Back then it seemed like such a big place, all bright lights and bridges. Compared to New York, though..."

When she didn't finish, Hogan said, "You and your husband met young, huh?"

And only then did Chloe realize just how much she had revealed. She hadn't meant to bring up Samuel again. Truly, she hadn't. But it was impossible to think about home without thinking of him, too. Strangely, though, somehow, thinking about him now wasn't quite as painful as it had been before.

"In high school," she heard herself say. "Freshman year. We married our sophomore year in college. I know that sounds like we were too young," she said, reading his mind this time—because everyone had thought marrying at twenty was too young. Everyone still thought that. For Chloe and Samuel, it had felt like the most natural thing in the world.

"How did he…?" Hogan began. "I mean…if you don't mind my asking… What happened?"

She expelled a soft sigh. Of course, she should have realized it would come to this sooner or later with Hogan. It was her own fault. She was the one who'd brought up her late husband. She couldn't imagine why. She never talked about Samuel with anyone. Ever. So why was she not minding talking about him to Hogan?

"Asymptomatic coronary heart disease," she said. "That's what happened. He had a bad heart. That no one knew about. Until, at twenty-two years of age, he had a massive heart attack that killed him while he was performing the physically stressful act of slicing peppers for *tastira*. It's a Tunisian dish. His specialty was Mediterranean cooking," she added for some reason. "We would have been an unstoppable team culinarily speaking, once we opened our restaurant."

Hogan was silent for a moment, then, very softly, he said, "Those are his chef's jackets you wear, aren't they?"

Chloe nodded. "After he was… After we sprinkled his ashes in Brown County, I realized I didn't have anything of him to keep with me physically. We didn't exchange rings when we married, and we weren't big on gift-giving." She smiled sadly. "Symbols of affection just never seemed necessary to either of us. So, after he was gone, I started wearing his jackets when I was cooking."

She had thought wearing Samuel's jackets would make her feel closer to him. But it hadn't. It wasn't his clothing that helped her remember him. If she'd needed physical reminders for that, she never would have left Indiana. But she'd been wearing them for so long now, it almost felt wrong to stop.

She reached for her wine and enjoyed a healthy taste of it. It warmed her mouth and throat as she swallowed, but it did nothing to combat the chill that suddenly enveloped her. So she put the glass down and wrapped her shawl more tightly around herself.

"I'm sorry, Chloe," Hogan said, his voice a soft caress in the darkness. "I shouldn't have asked for details."

"It's okay," she told him, even though it really wasn't okay. "It was a long time ago. I've learned to…cope with it. The money I make as a chef goes into a fund I started in Samuel's name that makes testing for the condition in kids less expensive, more common and more easily accessible. Knowing that someone else—maybe even a lot of someone elses—might live longer lives with their loved ones by catching their condition early and treating it helps me deal."

Hogan was being quiet again, so Chloe looked over to see how he was handling everything she'd said. He didn't look uncomfortable, though. Mostly, he looked sympathetic. He'd lost people he loved at a young age, too, so maybe he really did understand.

"I lied when I said the reason I came to New York was to open my own restaurant," she told him. "There's no way I could do that now, without Samuel. It was our dream together. I really came to New York because I thought it would be a good place to lose myself after he died. It's so big here, and there are so many people. I thought it would be easier than staying in a place where I was constantly reminded of him. And it's worked pretty well. As long as I'm able to focus on cooking, I don't have to think about what happened. At least I didn't until—"

She halted abruptly. Because she had been *this close* to telling Hogan it had worked pretty well until she met him. Meeting him had stirred up all sorts of feelings she hadn't experienced in years. Feelings she'd only ever had for one other human being. Feelings she'd promised herself she would never, ever, feel again. She'd barely survived losing Samuel. There was no way she could risk—no way she *would* risk—going through that again. No way she would ever allow someone to mean that much to her again. Not even—

"At least you did until I asked about it." Hogan finished her sentence for her. Erroneously, at that. "Wow. I really am a mook."

"No, Hogan, that's not what I was going to say." Before he could ask for clarification, however, she quickly concluded, "Anyway, that's what happened."

The temperature on the roof seemed to have plummeted since they first came outside, and a brisk wind riffled the potted flowers and rippled the lights overhead. Again, Chloe wrapped herself more snugly in her shawl. But the garment helped little. So she brought her knees up on the sofa and wrapped her arms around her legs, curling herself into as tight a ball as she could.

"You know how people say it's better to have loved and lost than to never have loved at all?" she asked.

"Yeah," Hogan replied softly.

"And you know how people say it's better to feel bad than to feel nothing at all?"

"Yeah."

"People are full of crap."

He paused before asking even more softly than before, "Do you really think that?"

She answered immediately. "Yes."

Hogan waited a moment before moving closer, dropping an arm across her shoulders and pulling her to him, tucking the crown of her head beneath his chin. Automatically, Chloe leaned into him, pressing her cheek to his shoulder, opening one hand over his chest. There was nothing inappropriate in his gesture or in her reaction to it. Nothing suggestive, nothing flirtatious, nothing carnal. Only one human being offering comfort to another. It had been a long time since anyone had held Chloe, even innocently. A long time since anyone had comforted her. And now here was Hogan, his heat enveloping her, his scent surrounding her, his heart thrumming softly beneath her palm. And for the first time in years—six years, nine months, one week and one day, to be precise—Chloe felt herself responding.

But there, too, lay problems. After Samuel's death, she'd lost herself for a while, seeking comfort from the sort of men who offered nothing but a physical release for the body and no comfort for the soul. The behavior had been reminiscent of her mother's—erratic and self-destructive—and when Chloe finally realized that, she'd reined herself in and shut herself up tight. Until tonight.

Suddenly, with Hogan, she did want holding. And she wanted comforting. And anything else he might have to offer. She reminded herself that his heart and his future were with someone else. He was planning a life with Anabel. But Chloe didn't want a future or a life with him. She'd planned a life once, and the person she'd planned it with was taken from her. She would never make plans like that again. But a night with Hogan? At the moment a night with him held a lot of appeal.

She tilted her head back to look at his face. His brown eyes were as dark as the night beyond, and the breeze ruffled his sandy hair, nudging a strand down over his forehead. Without thinking, Chloe lifted a hand to brush it back, skimming her fingers lightly along his temple after she did. Then she dragged them lower, tracing the line of his jaw. Then lower still, to graze the column of his throat. His pupils expanded as she touched him, and his lips parted.

Still not sure what was driving her—and, honestly, not really caring—she moved her head closer to his. Hogan met her halfway, brushing her lips lightly with his once, twice, three times, four, before covering her mouth completely. For a long time he only kissed her, and she kissed him back, neither of them shifting their position, as if each wanted to give the other the option of putting a stop to things before they went any further.

But neither did.

So Chloe threaded her fingers through his hair, cupped the back of his head in her palm and gave herself more fully to the kiss. At the same time, Hogan dropped his other hand to her hip, curving his fingers over her to pull her closer still. She grew ravenous then, opening her mouth against his, tasting him more deeply. When he pulled her into his lap, wrapping both arms around her waist, she looped hers around his neck and held on for dear life.

She had no idea how long they were entwined that way—it could have been moments, it could have been millennia. Chloe drove her hands over every inch of him she could reach, finally pushing her hand under the hem of his sweater. The skin of his torso was hot and hard and smooth beneath her fingertips, like silk-covered steel. She had almost forgotten how a man's body felt, so different from her own, and she took her time rediscovering. Hogan, too, went exploring, moving his hand from her hip to her waist to her breast. She cried out when he cupped his hand over her, even with the barrier of her sweater between them. It had just been so long since a man touched her that way.

He stilled his hand at her exclamation, but he didn't move it. He only looked at her with an unmistakable question in his eyes, as if waiting for her to make the next move. She told herself they should put a stop to things now. She even went so far as to say, "Hogan, we probably shouldn't…" But she was unable—or maybe unwilling—to say the rest. Instead, she told him, "We probably shouldn't be doing this out here in the open."

He hesitated. "So then…you think we should do this inside?"

Chloe hesitated a moment, too. But only a moment. "Yes."

He lowered his head to hers one last time, pressing his palm flat against her breast for a moment before dragging it back down to her waist. Then he was taking her hand in his, standing to pull her up alongside him. He kissed her again, long and hard and deep, then, his fingers still woven with hers, led her to the roof access door. Once inside the stairwell, they embraced again, Hogan pressing her back against the wall to crowd his body against hers, their kisses deepening until their mouths were both open wide. She drove her hands under his sweater again to splay them open against the hot skin of his back, and he dropped a hand between her legs, petting her over the fabric of her pants until she was pushing her hips harder into his touch.

Somehow they made it down the stairs to Hogan's bedroom. Somehow they made it through the door. Somehow they managed to get each other's clothes off. Then Chloe was naked on her back in his bed, and Hogan was naked atop her. As he kissed her, he dropped his hand between her legs again, growling his approval when he realized how damp and ready for him she already was. He took a moment to make her damper, threading his fingers through her wet flesh until she was gasping for breath, then he drew his hand back up her torso to her breast. He thumbed the ripe peak of one as he filled his mouth with the other, laving her with the flat of his tongue and teasing her with its tip. In response, Chloe wove her fingers together at his nape and hooked her legs around his waist as if she intended to hold him there forever.

Hogan had other plans, though. With one final, gentle tug of her nipple with his teeth, he began dragging openmouthed kisses back down along her torso. He paused long enough to taste the indentation of her navel then scooted lower still, until his mouth hovered over the heated heart of her. Then he pressed a palm against each of her thighs and pushed them open, wide enough that he could duck his head between them and taste the part of her he'd fingered long moments ago.

The press of his tongue against her there was almost more than Chloe could bear. She tangled her fingers in his hair in a blind effort to move him away, but he drove his hands beneath her fanny and pushed her closer to his mouth. Again and again, he darted his tongue against her, then he treated her to longer, more leisurely strokes. Something wild and wanton coiled tighter inside her with every movement, finally bursting in a white-hot rush of sensation that shook her entire body. Before the tremors could ebb, he was back at her breast, wreaking havoc there again.

After that Chloe could only feel and react. There were no thoughts. No cares. No worries. There was only Hogan and all the things he made her feel.

Hogan and all the things she wanted to do to him, too. When he finally lifted his head from her breast, she pulled him up to cover his mouth with hers, reaching down to cover the head of his shaft with her hand when she did. He was slick and hard, as ready for her as she was for him. But she took her time, too, to arouse him even more, palming him, wrapping her fingers around him, driving her hand slowly up and down the hard, hot length of him.

When he rolled onto his back to facilitate her movements, Chloe bent over him, taking as much of him into her mouth as she could. Over and over she savored him, marveling at how he swelled to even greater life. When she knew he was close to coming, she levered her body over his to straddle him, easing herself down over his long shaft then rising slowly up again. Hogan cupped his hands over her hips, guiding her leisurely up and down atop himself. But just as they were both on the verge of shattering, he reversed their bodies so that Chloe was on her back again. He grinned as he circled each of her ankles in strong fists, then he knelt before her and opened her legs wide. And then—oh, *then*—he was plunging himself into her as deep as he could go, thrusting his hips against hers again and again and again.

Never had she felt fuller or more complete than she did during those moments that he was buried inside her. Every time he withdrew, she jerked her hips upward to stop him, only to have him come crashing into her again. They came as one, both crying out in the euphoria that accompanied climax. Then Hogan collapsed, turning their bodies again until he was on his back and she was lying atop him. Her skin was slick and hot. Her brain was dazed and shaken. And her heart…

Chloe closed her eyes, refusing to complete the thought. There would be no completion of thought tonight. There would be completion only for the body. And although her body felt more complete than it had in a very long time, she already found herself wanting more.

Her body wanted more, she corrected herself. Only her body. Not her. But as she closed her eyes against the fatigue that rocked her, she felt Hogan press a kiss against the crown of her head. And all she could think was that, of everything he'd done to her tonight, that small kiss brought her the most satisfaction.

# Seven

Chloe awoke slowly to darkness. She hated waking up before the alarm went off at five, because she could never get back to sleep for that last little bit of much needed slumber. Invariably her brain began racing over the list of things she had to do that day, not stopping until she rose to get those things done. Strangely, though, this morning, her brain seemed to be sleepier than she was, because it wasn't racing at all. There were no thoughts bouncing around about the intricacies of the asparagus-brie soufflé she planned for this morning's breakfast. No reminders ricocheting here and there that her savory and marjoram plants were looking a little peaked, so she needed to feed them. No, there were only idle thoughts about—

Hogan. Oh, my God, she'd had sex with Hogan last night. Worse, she had woken up in his bed instead of her own. Now she would have to sneak out under cover of darkness before he woke up so she could get ready for work and make his breakfast, then figure out how to pretend like there was nothing different about this morning than any of the mornings that had preceded it and *Just have a seat in the dining room, Hogan, and I'll bring you your breakfast the way I always do, as if the two of us weren't just a few hours ago joined in the most intimate way two people can be joined.*

Oh, sure. *Now* her brain started working at light speed.

Thankfully, Mrs. Hennessey had weekends off, so Chloe didn't have to worry about explaining herself to the housekeeper. Even if Mrs. Hennessey did remind her of her grandmother, who Chloe could just imagine looking at her right now and saying with much disappointment, *"Mon petit doigt me dit..."* which was the French equivalent of "A little bird told me," a phrase Mémée never had to finish because as soon as she started to say it, Chloe would always break down in tears and confess whatever it was she'd done.

And now she'd *really* done it.

Panicked by all the new worries rioting in

her head, Chloe turned over, hoping to not wake Hogan. But the other side of the bed was empty. She breathed a sigh of relief...for all of a nanosecond, because her gaze then fell on the illuminated numbers of the clock on the nightstand beyond.

It was almost nine thirty! She never slept until nine thirty! Even on her days off! Which today wasn't!

By now she should have already finished cleaning up breakfast and should be sipping a cup of rose and lavender tea while she made a list for her afternoon shopping. She had completely missed Hogan's breakfast this morning. Never in her life had she missed making a meal she was supposed to make for an employer. How could she have slept so late?

The answer to that question came immediately, of course. She had slept so late because she was up so late. And she was up so late because she and Hogan had been... Well. Suffice it to say Hogan was a very thorough lover. He'd been even more insatiable than she.

Heat swept over her at some of the images that wandered into her brain. Hogan hadn't left an inch of her body untouched or untasted. And that last time they'd come together, when he'd turned her onto her knees and pressed her shoulders to the mattress, when he'd entered her more deeply than she'd ever felt entered before, when he threaded his fingers through her damp folds of flesh and curried them in time with the thrust of his shaft, then spilled himself hotly inside her...

Oh, God. She got hot all over again just thinking about it.

How could she have let this happen? She wished she could blame the wine. Or Hogan's unrelenting magnetism. Or the romance of New York at night. Anything besides her own weakness. But she knew she had only herself to blame. She had let her guard down. She had opened herself up to Hogan. She had allowed herself to feel. And she had lost another part of herself as a result.

No, not lost, she realized. She had surrendered herself this time. She had given herself over to Hogan willingly. And she would never be able to get that part of herself back.

She'd barely been able to hold it together after Samuel died. She'd had to tie herself up tight, hide herself so well that nothing outside would ever get to her again. Because losing something—someone— again might very well be the end of her.

She tried looking at it a different way. Okay, so she and Hogan had sex. So what? She'd had sex before. It was just sex. She'd been physically attracted to Hogan since the minute she met him. He was a very attractive man. Last night she'd simply acted on that attraction. As had he. But it was just an attraction. Hogan was in love with Anabel. He'd been in love with Anabel for nearly half his life. And

Chloe still loved her late husband. Just because she and Hogan had enjoyed a little—okay, a lot of—sex one night didn't mean either of them felt any differently about each other today. It was sex. Not love.

So why did everything seem different?

She had to get out of Hogan's room and back to her own so she could regroup and figure out what to do. She was fumbling for a lamp on the nightstand when the bedroom door opened, throwing a rectangle of light onto the floor and revealing Hogan standing before it. He was wearing jeans and nothing else, and his hair was still mussed from the previous night's activities. He was carrying a tray topped with a coffeepot and a plate whose contents she couldn't determine.

"You're awake," he said by way of a greeting, his voice soft and sweet and full of affection.

Chloe's stomach pitched to hear it. Affection wasn't allowed. Affection had no place in a physical reaction. No place in sex. No place in Chloe's life anywhere.

"Um, yeah," she said, pulling the covers up over her still-naked body. "I'm sorry I overslept. I can have your breakfast ready in—"

"I made breakfast," he interrupted.

Well, that certainly wasn't going to look good on her résumé, Chloe thought. Mostly because she was afraid to think anything else. Like how nice it was of Hogan to make breakfast. Or how sweet and earnest he sounded when he told her he had. Or the warm, fuzzy sensation that swept through her mid-section when he said it.

"I mean, it's not as good as what you would have made," he continued when she didn't respond. "But I didn't want to wake you. You were sleeping pretty soundly."

And still, she had no idea what to say.

Hogan made his way silently into the dim room. He strode first to the window and, balancing the tray in one hand, tugged open the curtains until a wide slice of sunlight spilled through. Then he smiled, scrambling Chloe's thoughts even more than they already were. When she didn't smile back—she couldn't, because she was still so confused by the turn of events—his smile fell. He rallied it again, but it wasn't quite the same.

When he set the tray at the foot of the bed, she saw that, in addition to the coffee, it held sugar and cream, along with a modest assortment of not-particularly-expertly-cut fruit, an array of not-quite-done to far-too-done slices of toast, some cheese left over from last night and a crockery pot of butter.

"I wasn't sure how you like your coffee," he said. "But I found cream in the fridge, so I brought that. And some sugar, just in case."

When Chloe still didn't reply, he climbed back into bed with her. But since it was a king-size, he was nearly as far away from her as he would have been in Queens. Even so, she tugged the covers up even higher, despite the fact that she had already pulled them as high as they would go without completely cocooning herself. Hogan noticed the gesture and looked away, focusing on the breakfast he'd made for them.

"It's weird," he said. Which could have referred to a lot of things. Thankfully, he quickly clarified, "You know what I like for every meal, but I don't even know what you like to have for breakfast. I don't even know how you take your coffee."

"I don't drink coffee, actually," she finally said.

He looked back at her. "You don't?"

She shook her head.

"Then why is there cream in the fridge?"

"There's always cream in the fridge when you cook French."

"Oh. Well. Then what do you drink instead of coffee?"

"Tea."

"If you tell me where it is, I could fix you—"

"No, that's okay."

"If you're sure."

"I am."

"So…what kind of tea?"

"Dragon tea. From Paris."

"Ah."

"But you can get it at Dean and DeLuca."

"Gotcha."

"I don't put cream in it, either."

"Okay."

"Or sugar."

"Noted."

The conversation—such as it was—halted there. Chloe looked at Hogan. Hogan looked at Chloe. She fought the urge to tug up the sheet again. He mostly just sat there looking gorgeous and recently tumbled. She told herself to eat something, reminded herself that it was the height of rudeness to decline food someone had prepared for you. But her stomach was so tied in knots, she feared anything she tried to put in it would just come right back up again.

Before she knew what she was doing, she said, "Hogan, about last night..." Unfortunately, the cliché was as far as she got before she realized she didn't know what else to say. She tried again. "What happened last night was..." At that, at least, she couldn't prevent the smile that curled her lips. "Well, it was wonderful," she admitted.

"I thought so, too."

Oh, she really should have talked faster. She really didn't need to hear that he had enjoyed it, too. Not that she didn't already know he'd enjoyed it. Especially considering how eagerly he'd—

Um, never mind.

She made herself say the rest of what she had hoped to get in before he told her he'd enjoyed last night, too, in case he said more, especially something about how eagerly he'd—

"But it never should have happened," she made herself say.

This time Hogan was the one to not say anything in response. So Chloe made an effort to explain. "I was feeling a little raw last night, talking about Samuel and things I haven't talked about to anyone for a long time. Add to that the wine and the night and New York and..." She stopped herself before adding *and you* and hurried on, "Things just happened that shouldn't have happened. That wouldn't have happened under normal circumstances. That won't happen again. You're my employer, and I'm your employee. I think we can both agree that we should keep it at that."

When he continued to remain silent, she added, "I just want you to know that I'm not assuming anything will come of it. I don't want you to think I'm under the impression that this—" here, she gestured quickly between the two of them "—changes that. I know it doesn't."

And still, Hogan said nothing. He only studied her thoughtfully, as if he was trying to figure it all out the same way she was.

*Good luck with that*, Chloe thought. Then again, maybe he wasn't as confused as she was. Maybe he'd awoken this morning feeling perfectly philosophical about last night. Guys were able to do that better than girls were, right? To compartmentalize things into brain boxes that kept them neatly separate from other things? Sex in one box and love in another. The present moment in one box and future years in another. He probably wasn't expecting anything more to come of last night, either, and he'd just been sitting here waiting for her to reassure him that that was how she felt, too.

So she told him in no uncertain terms—guys liked it when girls talked to them in no uncertain terms, right?—to make it perfectly clear, "I just want you to know that I don't have any expectations from this. Or from you. I know what happened between us won't go any further and that it will never happen again. I know you still love Anabel."

"And you still love Samuel," he finally said.

"Yes. I do."

He nodded. But his expression revealed nothing of what he might actually be feeling. Not that she wanted him to feel anything. The same way she wasn't feeling anything. She wasn't.

"You're right," he agreed. "About all of it. What happened last night happened. But it was no big deal."

Well, she didn't say *that*. Jeez. Oh, wait. Yes, she did. At least, she'd been thinking it before Hogan came in with breakfast. Looking and sounding all sweet and earnest and being so gorgeous and recently tumbled. Okay, then. It was no big deal. They were both on the same page.

She looked at the breakfast he'd prepared. She had thought getting everything about last night out in the open the way they had would make her feel better. But her stomach was still a tumble of nerves.

Even so, she forced a smile and asked, "Could you pass the toast, please?"

Hogan smiled back, but his, too, looked forced. "Sure."

He pulled up the tray from the foot of the bed until it was between them, and Chloe leaned over to reach for the plate of toast. But the sheet began to slip the moment she did, so she quickly sat up again, jerking it back into place.

"I should let you get dressed," Hogan said, rising from bed.

"But aren't you going to have any breakfast?"

"I had some coffee while I was making it. That'll hold me for a while. You go ahead." He started to back toward the door. "I have some things I need to do today anyway."

"Okay."

"And, listen, I'm pretty sure I won't be here for dinner tonight, so don't go to any trouble for me."

"But I was going to make *blanquette de veau*. From my grandmother's recipe."

"Maybe another time."

Before she could say anything else—not that she

had any idea what to say—he mumbled a quick "See ya," and was out the door, leaving Chloe alone.

Which was how she liked to be. She'd kept herself alone for six years now. Six years, nine months, one week and... And how many days? She had to think for a minute. Two. Six years, nine months, one week and two days, to be precise. Alone was the only way she could be if she hoped to maintain her sanity. Especially after losing her mind the way she had last night.

She was right. It shouldn't have happened.

As Hogan bent over the hood of Benny Choi's '72 Mustang convertible, he repeated Chloe's assertion in his head again. Maybe if he repeated it enough times, he'd start believing himself. Chloe had been spot-on when she said last night was a mistake. It had been a mistake. An incredibly erotic, unbelievably satisfying mistake, but a mistake all the same.

She was still in love with her husband. First love was a potent cocktail. Nothing could cure a hangover from that. Hell, Hogan knew that firsthand, since he was still punch-drunk in love with Anabel fifteen years after the fact. Right? Of course right. What happened between him and Chloe last night was just a byproduct of the feelings they had for other people, feelings they'd both had bottled up for too long. Chloe had been missing her husband last night. Hogan had been missing Anabel. So they'd turned to each other for comfort.

Stuff like that happened all the time. It really was no big deal. Now that they had it out of their systems, they could go back to being in love with the people they'd loved half their lives.

Except that Chloe couldn't go back to her husband. Not the way Hogan could go back to Anabel.

"Thanks for coming in to work, Hogan," Benny said when Hogan dropped the hood of his car into place. "Now that your dad's gone, you're the only guy I trust with my baby."

Benny and Hogan's father had been friends since grade school. With what was left of Hogan's mother's family living solidly in the Midwest, Benny was the closest thing to an uncle Hogan had here in town. He was thinning on top, thickening around the middle and wore the standard issue blue uniform of the New York transit worker, having just ended his shift.

"No problem, Benny," Hogan assured him. "Feels good to come in. I've been missing the work."

"Hah," the other man said. "If I came into the kind of money you did, I wouldn't even be in New York. I'd be cruising around the Caribbean. Then I'd be cruising around Mexico. Then Alaska. Then… I don't even know after that. But I sure as hell wouldn't have my head stuck under Benny Choi's Mach One, I can tell you that."

Hogan grinned. "To each his own."

They moved into Hogan's office so he could prepare Benny's bill. Which seemed kind of ridiculous since Hogan wasn't doing this for a living anymore, so there was no need to charge anyone for parts or labor. With the money he had, he could buy a whole fleet of Dempsey's Garages and still have money left over. He knew better than to tell Benny the work was on the house, though. Benny, like everyone else in Hogan's old neighborhood, always paid his way. Even so, he knocked off twenty percent and, when Benny noticed the discrepancy, called it his new "friends and family" rate.

Hogan sat in his office for a long time after Benny left, listening to the clamor of metal against metal as the other mechanics worked, inhaling the savory aroma of lubricant, remembering the heft of every tool. He couldn't give this up. A lot of people would think he was crazy for wanting to keep working in light of his financial windfall, but he didn't care. Hogan had been working in this garage for nearly two decades, most of it by his father's side. It was the only place he'd ever felt like himself. At least it had been until last night, when he and Chloe had—

A fleet of Dempsey's Garages, he thought again, pushing away thoughts of things that would never happen again. He actually kind of liked the sound of that. There were a lot of independent garages struggling in this economy. He could buy them up, put the money into them that they needed to be competitive, keep everyone employed who wanted to stay employed and give everything and everyone a new purpose. He could start here in the city and move outward into the state. Then maybe into another state. Then another. And another. This place would be his flagship, the shop where he came in to work every day.

And it would be a lot of work, an enterprise that ambitious. But Hogan always thrived on work. Being away from it was why he'd been at such loose ends since moving uptown. Why he'd felt so dissatisfied. Why his life felt like something was missing.

And that was another thing. He didn't have to live uptown. He could sell his grandfather's house. It didn't feel like home anyway, and it was way too big for one person. Of course, Hogan wouldn't be one person for much longer. He'd have Anabel. And, with any luck, at some point, a few rug rats to keep tabs on. Still, the Lenox Hill town house was just too much. It didn't suit Hogan. He and Anabel could find something else that they both liked. She probably wouldn't want to move downtown, though. Still, they could compromise somewhere.

The more Hogan thought about his new plans, the more he liked them. Funny, though, how the ones for the garage gelled in his brain a lot faster and way better than the ones for Anabel did. But that was just because he was sitting here in the garage right now, surrounded by all the things he needed for making plans like that. Anabel was still out there, waiting for him to make contact. But he'd be seeing her next weekend, thanks to Chloe's dinner party plans. Yeah, Hogan was *this close* to having everything he'd ever wanted.

Thanks to Chloe.

# Eight

A week later, Hogan stood in his living room, wondering why the hell he'd let Chloe arrange a dinner party for him. It was for Anabel, he reminded himself. This entire situation with Chloe had always been about winning back Anabel.

Despite his recent encounter with Chloe—which neither of them had spoken about again—that was still what he wanted. Wasn't it? Of course it was. He'd spent almost half his life wanting Anabel. She was his Holy Grail. His impossible dream. A dream that was now very possible. All Hogan had to do was play his cards right. Starting now, with the evening ahead. If he could just keep his mind off making love to Chloe—or, rather, having sex with Chloe—and focus on Anabel.

He still wasn't looking forward to the night ahead, but he was relieved there wasn't going to be a large group coming. Chloe had only invited Anabel and three other couples, two of whom were friends of Anabel's that Chloe had assured him it would be beneficial for him to know, and one of whom was Gus Fiver and his date.

Hogan realized he should have been the one to plan something, and he should have been the one who invited Anabel to whatever it was, and he should be in charge of it. He also realized it should just be him and Anabel, and not a bunch of other people, too.

So why hadn't he done that? He'd been living in his grandfather's house for a month now, plenty of time for him to figure out how things were done here and proceed accordingly where it came to pursuing the love of his life. But the only time he'd seen Anabel since ascending to his new social status had been the day she came over to try and lure Chloe back to work for her. He'd thought about asking her out a lot of times over the last few weeks. But he'd always hesitated. Because he wanted the occasion to be just right, he'd told himself, and he hadn't figured out yet what *just right* was with Anabel these days.

Back when they were teenagers, they'd had fun walking along the boardwalk on Rockaway Beach or bowling a few sets at Jib Lanes or downing a couple of egg creams at Pop's Diner. Nowadays, though… Call him crazy, but Hogan didn't see the Anabel of today doing any of those things. He just didn't know what the Anabel of today did like. And that was why he hadn't asked her out.

Tonight he would find out what she liked and he *would* ask her out. Just the two of them. By summer, he promised himself again, they would be engaged. Then they would live happily ever after, just like in the books.

"You're not wearing that, are you?"

Hogan spun around to see Chloe standing in the doorway, dressed from head to toe in stark chef's whites. He'd barely seen her since last weekend. She'd sped in and out of the dining room so fast after serving him his meals that he'd hardly had a chance to say hello or thank her.

Tonight her jacket looked like it actually fit, and she'd traded her crazy printed pants for a pair of white ones that were as starched and pressed as the rest of her. Instead of the usual spray of hair erupting from the top of her head, she had it neatly twisted in two braids that fell over each shoulder. In place of bright red lipstick, she wore a shade of pink that was more subdued.

This must be what passed for formal attire for her. Even though she'd promised him the evening wasn't going to be formal. He looked down at his own clothes, standard issue blue jeans, white shirt and a pair of Toms he got on sale. Everything was as plain and inoffensive as clothing got, and he couldn't think of a single reason why Chloe would object to anything he had on.

"You said it was casual," he reminded her.

"I said it was *business* casual."

He shrugged. "Guys in business wear stuff like this all the time."

"Not for business casual, they don't."

"What's the difference?"

She eyed his outfit again. "Blue jeans, for one thing." Before he could object, she hurried on, "Okay, *maybe* blue jeans would be okay for some business casual functions, but only if they're dark wash, and only by certain designers."

"Levi Strauss has been designing jeans since the nineteenth century," Hogan pointed out.

Chloe crossed her arms over her midsection. "Yeah, and the ones you have on look like they were in his first collection."

"It took me years to get these broken in the way I like."

"You can't wear them tonight."

"Why not?"

"Because they're not appropriate for—"

"Then what is appropriate?" he interrupted. He was really beginning to hate being rich. There were way too many rules.

She expelled a much put-upon sigh. "What about the clothes you wore to the wine-tasting that day? Those were okay."

"That guy who bumped into me spilled some wine on my jacket, and it's still at the cleaner's."

"But that was weeks ago."

"I keep forgetting to pick it up. I never wear it."

"Well, what else do you have?"

He looked at his clothes again. "A lot of stuff like this, but in different colors."

"Show me."

Hogan opened his mouth to object again. People would be showing up soon, and, dammit, what he had on was fine. But he didn't want to argue with Chloe. These were the most words they'd exchanged in a week, and the air was already crackling with tension. So he made his way toward the stairs with her on his heels—at a safe distance. He told himself he was only changing his clothes because he wanted to look his best for Anabel, not like the kid from Queens she'd chosen someone else over. He wanted to look like a part of her tribe. Because he was a part of her tribe now. Why did he keep trying to fight it?

He took the stairs two at a time until he reached the fourth floor, not realizing until he got there how far behind Chloe was. He hadn't meant to abandon her. He was just feeling a little impatient for some reason. When she drew within a few stairs of him, he headed for his bedroom and threw open the closet that was as big as the dining room in the house where he grew up. It had four rods—two on each side—for hanging shirts and suits and whatever, a low shelf on each side beneath those for shoes, and an entire wall of drawers on the opposite end. Every stitch of clothing Hogan owned didn't even fill a quarter of it. The drawers were pretty much empty, too.

Mrs. Hennessey had started clearing out his grandfather's suits and shoes before Hogan moved in and was in the process of donating them to a place that outfitted homeless guys and ex-cons for job interviews—something that probably had his grandfather spinning in his grave, an idea Hogan had to admit brought him a lot of gratification. But the housekeeper had left a few things on one side she thought might be of use to Hogan because he and his grandfather were about the same size. Hogan hadn't even looked through them. He just couldn't see himself decked out in the regalia of Wall Street, no matter how high he climbed on the social ladder.

Chloe hesitated outside the bedroom door for some reason, looking past Hogan at the room itself. The room that was furnished in Early Nineteenth Century Conspicuous Consumption, from the massive Oriental rug in shades of dark green, gold and rust to the leather sofa and chair in the sitting area, to the quartet of oil paintings of what looked like the same European village from four different angles, to the rows of model cars lining the fireplace mantel, to the mahogany bed and dressers more suited to a monarch than a mechanic.

Then he realized it wasn't so much the room she was looking at. It was the bed. The bed that, this time last week, they were only a few hours away from occupying together, doing things with and to each other that Hogan had barely ever even fantasized about. Things he'd thought about a lot since. Things, truth be told, he wouldn't mind doing again.

Except with Anabel next time, he quickly told himself. Weird, though, how whenever he thought about those things—usually when he was in bed on his back staring up at the ceiling—it was always Chloe, not Anabel, who was with him in his fantasies.

In an effort to take both their minds off that night, he said, "Yeah, I know, the room doesn't suit me very well, does it? Even the model cars are all antiques worth thousands of dollars—I Googled them—and not the plastic Revell kind I made when I was a kid. I didn't change anything, though, because I thought maybe I'd learn to like it. I haven't. Truth be told, I don't think I'll ever stop feeling like an outsider in this house."

He hated the rancor he heard in his voice. Talk about first world problems. Oh, boo-hoo-hoo, his house was too big and too luxurious for his liking.

Oh, no, he had millions of dollars' worth of antiques and collectibles he didn't know what to do with. How would he ever be able to deal with problems like that? Even so, being rich was nothing like he'd thought it would be.

"Then redecorate," Chloe said tersely.

"Oh, sure," he shot back. "God knows I have great taste, what with working under cars on a street filled with neon and bodegas and cement. Hell, apparently, I can't even dress myself."

She winced at the charge. "I didn't mean it like that."

"Didn't you?"

"No. I—"

Instead of explaining herself, she made her way in Hogan's direction, giving him a wide berth as she entered the closet.

"My stuff is on the left," he told her. "The other side is what's left of my grandfather's things."

He hadn't been joking when he told her everything he had was like what he had on, only in different colors. He'd never been much of a clotheshorse, and he didn't follow trends. When his old clothes wore out, he bought new ones, and when he found something he liked, he just bought it in a few different colors. He hadn't altered his blue jeans choice since he first started wearing them, and when he'd started wearing them, he just bought what his old man wore. If it came down to a life-or-death situation, Hogan could probably name a fashion designer. Probably. He just didn't put much thought into clothes, that was all.

Something that Chloe was obviously discovering, since she was pushing through his entire wardrobe at the speed of light and not finding a single thing to even hesitate over. When she reached the last shirt, she turned around and saw the drawers where he'd stowed his, um, drawers. Before he could stop her, she tugged open the one closest to her and thrust her hand inside, grabbing the first thing she came into contact with, which happened to be a pair of blue boxer-briefs. Not that Hogan cared if she saw his underwear, at least when he wasn't wearing it. And, yeah, okay, he wouldn't mind if she saw it while he was wearing it, either, which was something he probably shouldn't be thinking about when he was anticipating the arrival of his newly possible dream. So he only leaned against the closet door and crossed his arms over his midsection.

Chloe, however, once she realized what she was holding, blushed. Actually blushed. Hogan didn't think he'd ever seen a woman blush in his life. He'd never gone for the kind of woman who would blush. Especially over something like a guy's underwear that he wasn't even wearing.

"There are socks and T-shirts in the other drawers," he told her, hoping to spare her any more embarrassment. Not that there was anything that embarrassing about socks and T-shirts. Unless maybe it was the fact that he'd had some of them, probably, since high school. "But I'm thinking you probably wouldn't approve of a T-shirt for business casual, either."

She stuffed his underwear back where she found it and slammed the drawer shut. Then she looked at the clothes hanging opposite his. "Those belonged to your grandfather?"

"Yeah," Hogan told her. "Mrs. Hennessey is in the middle of donating all his stuff to charity."

Chloe made her way to the rows of shirts, pants and jackets lined up neatly opposite his own and began to give them the quick *whoosh-whoosh-whoosh* she'd given his. She was nearly to the end when she withdrew a vest and gave it a quick perusal.

"Here," she said, thrusting it at Hogan with one hand as she began to sift through a collection of neckties with the other.

He accepted it from her automatically, giving it more thorough consideration than she had. The front was made of a lightweight wool charcoal, and it had intricately carved black buttons he was going to go out on a limb and guess weren't plastic. The back was made out of what looked like a silk, gray-on-gray paisley. It was a nice enough vest, but he wasn't really the vest-wearing type.

In case she wasn't reading his mind, though, he said, "I'm not really the vest-wearing ty—"

"And put this on, too," she interrupted, extending a necktie toward him.

It, too, looked as if it was made of silk and was decorated with a sedate print in blues, greens and grays that complemented the vest well. It was nice enough, but Hogan wasn't really the tie-wearing type, either.

"I'm not really the tie-wearing ty—"

"You are tonight," Chloe assured him before he could even finish protesting.

As if wanting to prove that herself, she snatched the vest from its hanger, leaving the latter dangling from Hogan's fingers. Before he knew it, she was maneuvering one opening of the vest over both of those and up his arm then circling to his other side to bring the vest over his other arm. Then she flipped up the collar of his shirt, looped the tie around his neck and began to tie it.

She fumbled with the task at first, as if she couldn't remember how to tie a man's tie—that made two of them—but by her third effort, she seemed to be recovering. She was standing closer to him than she'd been in a week. Close enough that Hogan could see tiny flecks of blue in her green eyes and feel the heat of her body mingling with his. He could smell her distinctive scent, a mix of soap and fresh herbs and something else that was uniquely Chloe Merlin. He was close enough that, if he wanted to, he could dip his head to hers and kiss her.

Not surprisingly, Hogan realized he did want to kiss her. He wanted to do a lot more than kiss her, but he'd start there and see what developed.

"There," Chloe said, bringing his attention back to the matter at hand.

Which, Hogan reminded himself, was about getting ready for dinner with the woman he was supposed to be planning to make his wife. He shouldn't be trying to figure out his feelings for Chloe. He didn't have feelings for Chloe. Not the kind he had for Anabel.

Chloe gave the necktie one final pat then looked up at Hogan. Her eyes widened in surprise, and she took a giant step backward. "I need to get back to the kitchen," she said breathlessly.

Then she was speeding past him, out of the closet and out of his room. But not, he realized as he watched her go, out of his thoughts. Which was where she should be heading fastest.

Hogan was surprised at how much fun he had entertaining near-strangers in his still-strange-to-him home. The wife of one couple who was friends of Anabel's had been in the cab with her the night Hogan met her, so they shared some history there. The other couple who knew her was affable and chatty. Gus Fiver and his date both shared Hogan's love of American-made muscle cars, so there was some lively conversation there. And Anabel...

Yeah. Anabel. Anabel was great. But the longer the night went on, the more Hogan realized neither of them were the people who met on Jamaica Avenue a decade and a half ago. She was still beautiful. Still smart. Still fierce. But she wasn't the seventeen-year-old girl who flipped off a cabbie in the middle of Queens any more than Hogan was the seventeen-year-old kid who'd fallen for her.

All he could conjure up was a fondness for a girl he knew at a time in his life when the world was its most romantic. And he was reasonably sure Anabel felt the same way about him. They talked like old friends. They joked like old friends. But there were no sparks arcing between them. No longing looks. No flirtation.

It was great to see her again. He wouldn't mind bumping into her from time to time in the future. But his fifteen-year-long fantasy of joining his life to hers forever evaporated before Chloe even brought in the second course. Which looked like some kind of soup.

"*Bisque des tomates et de la citrouille,*" she announced as she ladled the first helping into the bowl in front of Anabel.

"Ooo, Chloe, I love your tomato pumpkin bisque," Anabel said, leaning closer to inhale the aroma. "Thyme and basil for sure, but I swear she puts lavender in it, too." She looked at Chloe and feigned irritation. "She won't tell me, though. Damn her."

Chloe murmured her thanks but still didn't give Anabel the information she wanted. Then she circled the table with speed and grace, filling the bowls of everyone present before winding up at Hogan's spot. When she went to ladle up some soup for him, though, her grace and speed deserted her. Not only did she have trouble spooning up a decent amount, but when she finally did, she spilled a little on the tablecloth.

"I am so sorry," she said as she yanked a linen cloth from over her arm to dab at the stain.

"Don't worry about it," Hogan told her. "It'll wash out."

"That's not the point. I shouldn't have done it."

He was about to tell her it was fine, but noticed her hand was shaking as she tried to clean up what she'd done. When he looked at her face, he saw that her cheeks were flushed the same way they'd been in the closet, when she was handling his underwear. Must be hot in the kitchen, he decided.

"It's okay," he said again. Then, to his guests—because he wanted to take their attention off Chloe—he added, "Dig in."

Everyone did, but when Hogan looked at Anabel, she had a funny expression on her face. She wasn't looking at him, though. She wasn't even looking at the soup she professed to love. She was looking at Chloe. After a moment her gaze fell on Hogan.

"Your soup's going to get cold," he told her.

She smiled cryptically. "Not with the heat in this room, it won't."

Hogan narrowed his eyes. Funny, but he'd been thinking it was kind of cool in here.

The soup was, like everything Chloe made, delicious. As were the three courses that followed it. Everyone was stuffed by the time they were finished with dessert, a pile of pastries filled with cream and dripping with chocolate sauce that Anabel said was her most favorite thing Chloe made. In fact, every course that came out, Anabel had claimed was her most favorite thing Chloe made. Clearly, Chloe was doing her best to help Hogan woo the woman he had mistakenly thought was the love of his life. He wasn't sure how he was going to break it to her that all her hard work had been for nothing.

"We should have coffee on the roof," Anabel declared after the last of the dishes were cleared away.

Everyone agreed that they should take advantage of what the weather guys were saying would be the last of the pleasantly cool evenings for a while in the face of some inclement, more November-worthy weather to come. Hogan ducked into the kitchen long enough to tell Chloe their plans then led his guests up to the roof garden.

The view was the same as it was a week ago, but somehow the flowers looked duller, the white lights overhead seemed dimmer and the cityscape was less glittery. Must be smoggier tonight. He and his guests made their way to the sitting area just as Chloe appeared from downstairs. For a moment Hogan waited for her to join them in conversation, and only remembered she was working when she crossed to open the dumbwaiter. From it, she removed a tray with a coffeepot and cups, and little bowls filled with sugar, cream, chocolate shavings and some other stuff that looked like spices. Evidently, even after-dinner coffee was different when you were rich.

As Chloe brought the tray toward the group, Anabel drew alongside Hogan and hooked her arm through his affectionately. He smiled down at her when she did, because it was so like what she had done when they were kids. That was where the similarity in the gesture ended, however, because her smile in return wasn't one of the sly, flirtatious ones she'd always offered him when they were teenagers, but a mild, friendly one instead. Even so, she steered him away from his guests as Chloe began to pour the coffee, guiding him toward the part of the roof that was darkest, where the lights of the city could be viewed more easily. He didn't blame her. It was a really nice view. Once there, she leaned her hip against the balustrade and unlooped her arm from his. But she took both of his hands in hers and met his gaze intently.

"So how are you adjusting to Park Avenue life?" she asked, her voice low enough that it was clear she meant the question for him alone.

"I admit it's not what I thought it would be," he replied just as quietly. "But I guess I'll get used to it. Eventually."

He looked over at his other guests to make sure he wasn't being a neglectful host, but they were all engaged in conversation. Except for Chloe, who was busying herself getting everything set out on the table to her liking. And also sneaking peeks at Hogan and Anabel.

She was more concerned about the success of the evening than he'd been. He wished there was some way to signal her not to worry, that the evening had been a huge success, because he knew now the plans he'd made for the future weren't going to work out the way he'd imagined, and that was totally okay.

"I know it's a lot different from Queens," Anabel said, bringing his attention back to her. She was still holding his hands, but she dropped one to place her palm gently against his chest. "But Queens will always be here in your heart. No one says you have to leave it behind." She smiled. "In fact, I, for one, would be pretty mad at you if you did leave Queens behind. You wouldn't be Hogan anymore if you did."

"That will never happen," he assured her. "But it's still weird to think that, technically, this is the life I was born to."

She tipped her head to one side. "You have something on your cheek," she said.

Again? Hogan wanted to say. First the engine

grease with Chloe, now part of his dinner with Anabel. Before he had a chance to swipe whatever it was away, Anabel lifted her other hand to cup it over his jaw, stroking her thumb softly over his cheekbone.

"Coffee?"

He and Anabel both jumped at the arrival of Chloe, who seemed to appear out of nowhere. Anabel looked guilty as she dropped her hand to her side, though Hogan had no idea what she had to feel guilty about. Chloe looked first at Hogan, then at Anabel, then at Hogan again. When neither of them replied, she extended one cup toward Anabel.

"I made yours with cinnamon and chocolate," she said. Then she paraphrased the words Anabel had been saying all night. "I know it's your *most favorite*."

Hogan wasn't sure, but the way she emphasized those last two words sounded a little sarcastic.

"And, Hogan, yours is plain," Chloe continued. "Just the way I know *you* like it."

That, too, sounded a little sarcastic. Or maybe caustic. He wasn't sure. There was definitely something off about Chloe at the moment, though. In fact, there'd been something off about Chloe all night. Not just the soup-spilling when she'd ladled up his, but every course seemed to have had something go wrong, and always with Hogan's share of it. His *coq au vin* had been missing the *vin*, his *salade Niçoise* had been a nice salad, but there had hardly been any of it on his plate, his cheese course had looked like it was arranged by a five-year-old, and his cream puff dessert had been light on the cream, heavy on the puff.

He understood that, as the host, he was obligated to take whichever plates weren't up to standards, and he was fine with that. But that was just it—Chloe was *always* up to standards. She never put anything on the table that wasn't perfect. Until tonight.

Hogan and Anabel both took their coffee and murmured their thanks, but Chloe didn't move away. She only kept looking at them expectantly. So Hogan, at least, sipped from his cup and nodded.

"Tastes great," he said. "Thanks again."

Anabel, too, sampled hers, and smiled her approval. But Chloe still didn't leave.

So Hogan said, "Thanks, Chloe."

"You're welcome," Chloe replied. And still didn't leave.

Hogan looked at Anabel to see if maybe she knew why Chloe was still hanging around, but she only sipped her coffee and gazed at him with what he could only think were laughing eyes.

"So your coffee is all right?" Chloe asked Anabel.

"It's delicious," Anabel told her. "As you said. My *most favorite*. Somehow, tonight, it's even better than usual." She hesitated for the briefest moment then added, "Must be the company."

Even in the dim light, Hogan could see two bright

spots of pink appear on Chloe's cheeks. Her lips thinned, her eyes narrowed and her entire body went ramrod straight.

"I'm so happy," she said in the same crisp voice. Then she looked at Hogan. "For both of you."

Then she spun on her heels and went back to his other guests. Once there, however, she turned again to study Hogan and Anabel. A lot.

"What the hell was that about?" Hogan asked Anabel.

She chuckled. "You really have no idea, do you?"

He shook his head. "No. Is it some woman thing?"

Now Anabel smiled. "Kind of."

"Should I be concerned?"

"Probably."

Oh, yeah. This was the Anabel Hogan remembered. Cagey and evasive and having fun at his expense. Now that he was starting to remember her without the rosy sheen of nostalgia, he guessed she really could be kind of obnoxious at times when they were teenagers. Not that he hadn't been kind of obnoxious himself. He guessed teenagers in general were just kind of annoying. Especially when their hormones were in overdrive.

He studied Anabel again, but she just sipped her coffee and looked amused. "You're not going to tell me what's going on with Chloe, are you?" he asked.

"No."

"Just tell me if whatever it is is permanent, or if

she'll eventually come around and things can get back to normal."

She smiled again. "Hogan, I think I can safely say your life is never going to be normal again."

"I know, right? This money thing is always going to be ridiculous."

"I didn't mean the money part."

"Then what did you mean?"

She threw him another cryptic smile. "My work here is done." As if to punctuate the statement, she pushed herself up on tiptoe to kiss his cheek then told him, "Tonight was really lovely, Hogan. And illuminating."

Well, on that, at least, they could agree.

"Thank you for inviting me," she added. "But I should probably go."

"I'll walk you out."

"No, don't leave your guests. I can find my own way." She looked thoughtful for a moment before nodding. "In fact, I'm really looking forward to finding my own way in life for once."

She walked back toward the others. He heard her say her goodbyes and thank Chloe one last time, then she turned to wave to Hogan. As he lifted a hand in return, she strode through the door to, well, find her own way. Leaving Hogan to find his own way, too.

He just wished he knew where to go from here.

# Nine

Tonight was a disaster.

Chloe was still berating herself about it even as she dropped the last utensil into the dishwasher. There was just no way to deny it. The evening had been an absolute, unmitigated disaster. And not just the dinner party, where every single course had seen some kind of problem. The other disaster had been even worse. Hogan's reunion with Anabel had been a huge success.

Chloe tossed a cleaning pod into the dishwasher, sealed the door and punched a button to turn it on. It whirred to quiet life, performing perfectly the function for which it had been designed. She wished she could seal herself up just as easily then flip a switch to make herself work the way she was supposed to. She used to be able to do that. She did that as efficiently and automatically as the dishwasher did for six years. Six years, nine months and…and…

She leaned back against the counter and dropped her head into her hands. Oh, God. She couldn't remember anymore how many weeks or days to add to the years and months since Samuel's death. What was wrong with her?

And why had it hurt so much to see Hogan and Anabel together tonight? Chloe had known since the day she started working for Hogan that his whole reason for hiring her had been to find a way back into Anabel's life. He'd never made secret the fact that he still wanted the girl of his dreams fifteen years after they broke up, nor the fact that he was planning a future with her.

For Pete's sake, Chloe was the one who had been so adamant about throwing the dinner party tonight so the two of them would finally be in the same room together. She'd deliberately chosen all of Anabel's favorite dishes. She'd helped Hogan make himself more presentable for the woman he'd loved half his life so he could make a good impression on her.

And she'd accomplished her goal beautifully, because the two of them had laughed more than Chloe had ever seen two people laugh, and they'd engaged in constant conversation. They'd even wandered off as the evening wound down to steal some alone time together on the roof. Alone time Anabel had used to make clear that her interest in Hogan was as alive as it had ever been.

Chloe didn't think she'd ever be able to rid her brain of the image of Anabel splaying one hand open on Hogan's chest while she caressed his face with the other, the same way Chloe had done a week ago when she and Hogan were on the roof themselves. She knew what it meant when a woman touched a man that way. It meant she was halfway in love with him.

No! She immediately corrected herself. That wasn't what it meant. At least not where Chloe was concerned.

She started wiping down the kitchen countertops, even though she'd already wiped them off twice. You could never be too careful. She wasn't in love with Hogan. Not even halfway. She would never be in love with anyone again. Loving someone opened you up to too many things that could cause pain. Terrible, terrible, *terrible* pain. Chloe never wanted to hurt like that again. Chloe never *would* hurt like that again. She just wouldn't.

She wasn't in love with Hogan. She would never fall in love again.

Anyway, it didn't matter, because Hogan and Anabel were back on the road to the destiny they'd started when they were teenagers. His hiring of

Chloe had had exactly the outcome he'd intended. He'd won the woman of his dreams.

Before long Chloe would be cooking for two. She'd serve Hogan and Anabel their dinner every night, listening to their laughter and their fond conversation as they talked about their shared past and their plans for the future. And she'd bring in their breakfast every morning. Of course, Anabel liked to have breakfast in bed most days. She'd probably want that for her and Hogan both now. So Chloe would also be able to see them every morning all rumpled from sleep. And sex. More rumpled from sex than from sleep, no doubt, since Hogan's sexual appetites were so—

Well. She just wouldn't think about his sexual appetites anymore, would she? She wouldn't think about Hogan at all. Except in the capacity of him as her employer. Which was all he was. That was all he had ever been. It was all he would ever be. Chloe had reiterated that to him a week ago. All she had to do was keep remembering that. And forget about the way he—

She closed her eyes to shut out the images of her night with Hogan, images that had plagued her all week. But closing her eyes only brought them more fiercely into focus. Worse, they were accompanied by feelings. Again. Feelings she absolutely did not want to feel. Feelings she absolutely could not feel.

Feelings she absolutely would not feel. Not if she wanted to stay sane.

She finished cleaning up the kitchen and poured what was left of an open bottle of wine into a glass to take upstairs with her. As she topped the step to the fifth and highest floor of Hogan's house, her gaze inevitably fell on the roof access door across from her. Unable to help herself, she tiptoed toward it and cracked it open to see if anyone was still up there. She'd been surprised that Anabel left first, until she remembered her former employer often turned in early on Saturday night because she rose early on Sunday to drive to a farm in Connecticut where she stabled her horses.

There were still a few voices coming from the roof—Chloe recognized not just Hogan's, but Mr. Fiver's and his date's, as well. She wondered briefly if she should go up and check on the coffee situation then decided against it. She'd sent up a fresh pot and its accoutrements before cleaning up the kitchen, and Hogan had assured her he wouldn't need anything else from her tonight.

Or any other night, she couldn't help thinking as she headed for her room. He had Anabel to take care of any nightly needs he'd have from now on. And every other need he would ever have again. Which was good. It was. Chloe was glad things had worked out between the two former lovers the way they had. She was. Hogan would be happy now. And Anabel was a nice person. She also deserved to be happy. Now Chloe could focus completely on her cooking, which would make her happy, too. It would.

Happiness was bursting out all over. They were all hip deep in happiness. Happy, happy, happy. Yay for happiness.

Thank God she had the next two days off.

Hogan had always loved Sundays. Sunday was the one day of the week Dempsey's Parts and Service was closed—unless there was an emergency. He loved Sunday mornings especially, because he could sleep late and rise when he felt like it, then take his time eating something for breakfast that he didn't have to wolf down on the run, the way he did during the work week.

At least, that had always been the case before he became filthy, stinking rich. Over the course of the past month, though, Sundays hadn't been like they used to be. He hadn't been working his regular shifts at the garage, so how could one day differ from any other? And he didn't have to eat on the run anymore, so a leisurely Sunday breakfast was no different from any other breakfasts during the no-longer-work-week. No, he hadn't been completely idle since leaving Queens, but he hadn't had a regular schedule to keep. He hadn't had places he *had* to be or things he *had* to get done. Yeah, he was putting plans into place that would bring work and purpose back into his life, but there was no way his life—or his Sundays—would ever go back to being the way they were before.

The thing that had really made Sundays even less enjoyable than they were before, though, was that Chloe was never around on Sundays. She never stayed home on her days off, and the house felt even more alien and unwelcoming when she wasn't in it.

This morning was no different. Except that, somehow, it felt different. When Hogan stumbled into the kitchen in his usual jeans and sweater the way he did every Sunday morning to make coffee, the room seemed even more quiet and empty than usual. He busied himself making his usual bacon and eggs, but even eating that didn't pull him out of his funk.

Too little sleep, he decided. Gus Fiver and his date had hung around until the wee hours, so Hogan had logged half the amount of shut-eye he normally did. Of course, last weekend he'd woken having only logged a few hours of shut-eye, too, and he'd felt *great* that day. At least until Chloe had told him what a mistake the night before had been.

He stopped himself there. Chloe. What was he going to do about Chloe? The only reason he'd hired her was because he wanted to insinuate himself into Anabel's life. And the only reason he'd planned to keep her employed in the future was because she was Anabel's favorite chef. Not that he intended to fire her now—God, no—but her reason for being in his house had suddenly shifted. Hell, the whole dynamic of her place in his house seemed to have suddenly shifted. Hogan for sure still wanted Chloe around. But he didn't want her around because of Anabel anymore. He wanted Chloe around because of, well, Chloe.

He liked Chloe. He liked her a lot. Maybe more than liked her. All week he'd been thinking about Chloe, not Anabel. Even before he realized his thing for Anabel wasn't a thing anymore, it was Chloe, not Anabel, who had been living in his head. He'd had dozens of nights with Anabel in the past, and only one night with Chloe. But when he piled all those nights with Anabel into one place and set the single night with Chloe in another, that single night had a lot more weight than the dozens of others. He wanted to have more nights with Chloe. He wanted countless nights with Chloe. The problem was Chloe didn't want any more nights with him. She'd made that crystal clear.

And there was still the whole employer-employee thing. He didn't want Chloe as an employee any-more. He wanted her as…something else. He just wasn't sure what. Even by the time he finished his breakfast and was trying to decide what to do with his day—other than think about Chloe, since that would be a given—Hogan had no idea what to do about her. Even after cleaning up from his dinner that evening, he still didn't know what to do about her.

Chloe evidently did, though, because she came into the den Sunday night, where Hogan was putting together a preliminary plan for a state-wide chain of Dempsey's Garages, and handed him a long, white envelope.

"Here," she said as she extended it toward him.

She was dressed in street clothes, a pair of snug blue jeans and a voluminous yellow turtleneck, her hair in a ponytail, her glasses sliding down on her nose—which she pushed up with the back of her hand, so he knew she was feeling anxious about something.

"What is it?" he asked.

"My two weeks' notice."

He recoiled from the envelope as if she were handing him a rattlesnake. "What?"

"It's my two weeks' notice," she repeated. "Except that I'm taking advantage of article twelve, paragraph A, subheading one in my contract, and it's really my two days' notice."

Now Hogan stood. But he still didn't take the envelope from her. "Whoa, whoa, whoa. You can't do that."

"Yes, I can. That paragraph outlines my right to an immediate abdication of my current position in the event of force majeure."

His head was still spinning from her announcement, but he found the presence of mind to point out, "Force majeure only applies to things beyond our control like wars or strikes or natural disasters."

"Exactly," she said.

He waited for her to clarify whatever was beyond their control, but she didn't elaborate. So he asked, "Well, what's the force majeure that's making you give me your two weeks'—correction, two days'—notice?"

She hesitated, her gaze ricocheting from his to the shelves of books behind him. Finally, she said, "Impracticability."

Hogan narrowed his eyes. "Impracticability? What the hell does that mean?"

"It's a legitimate legal term. Look it up. Now, if you'll excuse me, I have a cab waiting."

"Wait, what? You're leaving right now? That's not two days' notice, that's two minutes' notice."

"Today isn't over yet, and tomorrow hasn't started," she said. "That's two days. And my new employers have a place ready for me, so there's no reason for me to delay starting."

She still wasn't looking at him. So he took a step to his left to put himself directly in her line of vision. As soon as he did, she dropped her gaze to the floor.

"You already have a new employer?" he asked.

"Yes."

Of course she already had a new employer. Since she'd come to work for him, Hogan had had to fend off a half dozen attempts from people besides Anabel to hire her away from him, upping her salary even more every time. He hadn't minded, though, especially now that he knew where the money went. He would have done anything to keep Chloe employed so he could keep himself on Anabel's radar. At least, that was what he'd been telling himself all those times. Now he knew there was another reason he'd wanted to keep Chloe on. He just still wasn't sure he knew how to put it in words.

"Who's your new employer?" he asked.

"I'm not required to tell you that," she replied, still looking at the floor.

"You might do it as a professional courtesy," he said, stalling. "Or even a personal one."

"It's no one you know."

"Chloe, if it's a matter of money, I can—"

"It isn't the money."

She still wasn't looking at him. So he tried a new tack.

"Haven't your working conditions here been up to standard?"

"My working conditions here have been—" She halted abruptly then hurried on, "My working conditions here have been fine."

"Well, if it isn't the money, and it isn't the working conditions, was it…" He hated to think it might be what he thought it was, but he had to know for sure. "Was it the taco meatloaf?"

She looked up at that, but she closed her eyes and shook her head.

Even though he'd assured her he wouldn't mention it again, he asked, "Then was it what happened after the taco meatloaf?"

Now she squeezed her eyes tight. "I have to go," she said again.

Hogan had no idea how to respond to that. She hadn't said specifically that it was their sexual encounter making her situation here "impracticable"— whatever the hell that was—but her physical reaction to the question was a pretty good indication that that was exactly what had brought this on. Why had she waited a week, though? If their hookup was what was bothering her, then why hadn't she given her notice last weekend, right after it happened?

He knew the answer immediately. Because of Anabel. Chloe had promised before they ended up in his bed that she would arrange a dinner party for him so he could spend time with Anabel and cinch their reconciliation. She'd stayed long enough to fulfill that obligation so Hogan would be able to reunite with the woman he'd professed to be in love with for half his life. Now she figured he and Anabel were on their way to their happily-ever-after, so there was no reason for her to hang around anymore. And, okay, he supposed it could get kind of awkward if Anabel reentered his life after he and Chloe had had sex. Maybe Chloe just wanted to avoid a scenario like that. His anxiety eased. If that was the case, it wasn't a problem anymore.

"Anabel and I aren't going to be seeing each other," he said.

At that, Chloe finally opened her eyes and met his gaze. This time she was the one to ask, "What do you mean?"

Hogan lifted his shoulders and let them drop. "I mean we're not going to be seeing each other. Not like dating anyway. We might still see each other as friends."

"I don't understand."

Yeah, that made two of them. Hogan tried to explain anyway. "Last night she and I both realized there's nothing between us now like there was when we were kids. No sparks. No fireworks. Whatever it was she and I had fifteen years ago, we've both outgrown it. Neither one of us wants to start it up again."

"But you've been pining for her for half your life."

This part, at least, Hogan had figured out. He told Chloe, "No, the seventeen-year-old kid in me was pining for her. I just didn't realize how much that kid has grown up in the years that have passed, and how much of his youthful impulses were, well, impulsive. The thirty-three-year-old me wants something else." He might as well just say the rest. He'd come this far. "The thirty-three-year-old me wants some*one* else."

Okay, so maybe that wasn't exactly saying the rest. He was feeling his way here, figuring it out as he went. Chloe, however, didn't seem to be following him. So Hogan pushed the rest of the words out of his brain and into his mouth. And then he said them aloud.

"He wants you, Chloe. *I* want you."

He had thought the announcement would make her happy. Instead, she recoiled like he'd hit her.

But all she said was, "You can't."

Now Hogan was the one who felt like he'd been hit. Right in the gut. With a two-by-four. But he responded honestly, "Too late. I do."

Her brows arrowed downward, and she swallowed hard. "I can't get involved with you, Hogan."

"Why not?"

"I can't get involved with anyone."

"But last weekend—"

"Last weekend never should have happened," she interrupted.

"But it did happen, Chloe. And you'll never convince me it didn't have an effect on you, the same way it had an effect on me. A big one."

"Oh, it definitely had an effect on me," she assured him. Though her tone of voice indicated she didn't feel anywhere near as good about that effect as he did.

"Then why—"

"Because I can't go there, Hogan. Ever again. I

was in love once, and it nearly destroyed me. I never want to love anyone like that again."

"Chloe—"

"You've experienced loss," she interrupted him. "With both of your parents. You know how much it hurts when someone you love isn't there for you anymore."

He nodded. "Yeah, but—"

"Now take that pain and multiply it by a hundred," she told him. "A thousand. As terrible as it is to lose a parent or a grandparent, it's even worse when you lose the person you were planning to spend the rest of your life with. Losing someone like that is so... It's..."

Tears filled her eyes, spilling freely as she continued. "Or even if you lose someone like that in old age, after the two of you have built a life together, you still have a lifetime worth of memories to get you through it, you know? You have your children to comfort you. Children who carry a part of that person inside them. Maybe they have their father's smile or his way of walking or his love of cardamom or something else that, every time you see it, it reminds you he's not really gone. Not completely. A part of him lives on in them. You walk through the house the two of you took years making your own, and you're reminded of dozens of Thanksgivings and Christmases and birthdays that were celebrated there. You have an *entire life* lived with that person to look back on. But when that person is taken from you before you even have a chance to build that life—"

She took off her glasses with one hand and swiped her eyes with the other. "It's a theft of your life before you even had a chance to live it," she said. "The children you planned to have with that person die, too. The plans you made, the experiences you should have shared, the memories you thought you'd make… All of that dies with him.

"A loss like that is overwhelming, Hogan. It brings with it a grief that goes so deep and is so relentless, you know it will never, ever, go away, and you know you can never, ever, grieve like that again. *I* can never grieve like that again. And the only way to avoid grieving like that again is to never love like that again. I have to go before I'm more—"

She halted abruptly, covering her eyes with both hands. Hogan had no idea how to respond to everything she'd said. As bad as it had been to lose his folks, he couldn't imagine losing someone he loved as much as Chloe had loved her husband. He hadn't loved anyone as much as she had loved her husband. Not yet anyway. But even after everything she'd just said—hell, because of everything she'd just said—he'd like to have the chance to find out what it *was* like to love someone that much. And if Chloe's last few words and the way she'd stopped short were any indication, maybe there was still a chance she might love that way again, too.

"I'm sorry, Chloe," he said. The sentiment was overused and of little comfort, but he didn't know what else to say. "Your husband's death was a terrible thing. But you can't stop living your life because something terrible happened. You have to do your best to move on and make a different life instead. You can't just shut yourself off from everything."

"Yes, I can."

He shook his head. "No. You can't. And you haven't."

She arrowed her brows down in confusion. "How do you know?"

He shrugged and smiled gently. "Because I think you pretty much just told me you love me."

"No, I didn't," she quickly denied. Maybe too quickly. "I don't love anyone. I'll never love anyone again. I can't."

"You mean you won't."

"Fine. I won't love anyone again."

"You think you can just make a choice like that? That by saying you won't love someone, it will keep you from loving them?"

"Yes."

"You really believe that?"

"I have to."

"Chloe, we need to talk more about this. A lot more."

"There's nothing to talk about," she assured him. Before he could object, she hurried on, "I'm sorry to leave you in the lurch. My letter includes a number of recommendations for personal chefs in the area who would be a good match for your culinary needs. Thank you for everything."

And then she added that knife-in-the-heart word that Anabel had never said to him when they were kids, the one word that would have let Hogan know it was over for good and never to contact her again, the word that, left unsaid the way it was then, had given him hope for years.

"Goodbye."

And wow, that word really did feel like a knife to the heart. So much so that he couldn't think of a single thing to say that would counter it, a single thing that would stop Chloe from leaving. All he could do was watch her rush out the door and head for the stairs. And all he could hear was her last word, with all its finality, echoing in his brain.

# Ten

Chloe stood in the kitchen of Hugo and Lucie Fleury, marveling again—she'd made herself marvel about this every day for the last three weeks—at what a plumb position she had landed. Her new situation was perfect for her—something else she made herself acknowledge every day—because Hugo and Lucie had grown up in Paris and arrived in New York for his new job only a year ago, so they were about as Parisian as a couple could be outside the City of Light. They didn't question anything Chloe put on the table, so she never had to explain a dish to them, their Central Park West penthouse was decorated in a way that made her feel as if she were living at Versailles and she was using her second language of French every day, so there was no chance of her getting rusty. *Mais oui*, all Chloe could say about her new assignment was, *C'est magnifique!*

So why didn't she feel so *magnifique* after almost a month of working here? Why did she instead feel so blasé? More to the point, why hadn't a single meal she'd created for the Fleurys come out the way it was supposed to? Why had everything she put together been a little…off? And now she was about to undertake a dinner party for twelve, the kind of challenge to which she normally rose brilliantly, and all she could do was think about the last dinner party she'd put together, and how it had resulted in—

Not that the Fleurys had complained about her performance, she quickly backtracked. They'd praised everything she set in front of them, and tonight's menu was no exception. Not that they'd tasted any of it yet, but, as Lucie had told her this morning, *"Ne vous inquiétez pas, Chloe. J'ai foi en vous."* Don't worry, Chloe. I have faith in you.

Well, that made one of them.

Lucie and Hugo didn't seem to realize or care that they were paying her more than they should for a party they could have had catered for less by almost any bistro, brasserie or café in New York. But Chloe realized they were doing that. And in addition to making her feel guilty and inadequate, it was driving her crazy. She just hadn't been at her best since leaving Hogan's employ. And the whole reason she'd left Hogan's employ was because she'd feared losing her ability to be at her best.

Well, okay, maybe that wasn't really the reason she'd left Hogan. But she was beginning to wonder if she'd ever be at her best again.

He'd called her every day the first week after she left, but she'd never answered. So he'd left messages, asking her to meet him so they could talk, even if it meant someplace public, because even though he didn't understand her desire to not tell him where she was working now, he respected it, and *C'mon, Chloe, pick up the phone, just talk to me, we need to figure this out.* As much as she'd wanted to delete the messages without even listening to them, something had compelled her to listen…and then melt a little inside at the sound of his voice. But even after hearing his messages, she still couldn't bring herself to delete them. Deleting Hogan just felt horribly wrong. Even if she never intended to see him again.

I *want you.*

The words he said the night she left still rang in her ears. She wanted Hogan, too. It was why she couldn't stay with him. Because wanting led to loving. And loving led to needing. And needing someone opened you up to all kinds of dangers once that person was gone. Losing someone you needed was like losing air that you needed. Or water. Or food. Without those things, you shriveled up and died.

*I think you pretty much just told me you love me.*

Those words, too, wouldn't leave her alone. Because yes, as much as she'd tried to deny it, and as much as she'd tried to fight it, she knew she loved Hogan. But she didn't need him. She wouldn't need him. She couldn't need him. And the only way to make sure of that was to never see him again.

Unfortunately, the moment Chloe entered the Fleurys' salon in her best chef's whites with a tray of canapés, she saw that her determination to not see Hogan, like so many other things in life, was completely out of her control. The Fleurys had invited him to their dinner party.

Or maybe they'd invited Anabel, she thought when she saw her other former employer at Hogan's side, and he was her plus-one. Whatever the case, Chloe was suddenly in the same room with him again, and that room shrank to the size of a macaron the moment she saw him. He was wearing the same shirt with the same vest and tie she'd picked out for him the night of his own dinner party, but he'd replaced his battered Levi's with a pair of pristine dark wash jeans that didn't hug his form nearly as well.

As if he'd sensed her arrival the moment she noted his, he turned to look at her where she stood rooted in place. Then he smiled one of his toe-curling, heat-inducing smiles and lifted a hand in greeting. All Chloe wanted to do then was run back into the kitchen and climb into a cupboard and forget she ever saw him. Because seeing him only reminded her how much she loved him. How much she wanted him. How much—dammit—she needed him.

Instead, she forced her feet to move forward and into the crowd. Miraculously, she made it without tripping or sending a canapé down anyone's back. Even more astonishing, she was able to make eye contact with Hogan when she paused in front of him and Anabel. But it was Anabel who broke the silence that settled over them.

"Oh, yum. *Brie gougères*. Chloe, I absolutely love your *brie gougères*." She scooped up two and smiled. "I love them so much, I need to take one over to Hillary Thornton. Talk amongst yourselves."

And then she was gone, leaving Chloe and Hogan alone for the first time in almost a month. Alone in the middle of a crowd of people who were waiting to try her *brie gougères* and her *choux de Bruxelles citrons* and the half dozen other hors d'oeuvres she'd prepared for the evening. None of which had turned out quite right.

"Hi," he said softly.

"Hello," she replied.

"How've you been?"

"All right." The reply was automatic. Chloe had been anything but all right since she last saw him. The same way her food had been anything but all right. The same way life itself had been anything but all right.

They said nothing more for a moment, only stood in the middle of a room fit for a king, as nervous as a couple of teenagers on their first date.

Finally, Hogan said, "What are you doing after the party?"

Again, Chloe replied automatically. "Cleaning up the kitchen."

He grinned, and Chloe did her best not to have an orgasm on the spot. "What about after that?" he asked.

"I'll, um… I'll probably have a glass of wine."

"Want some company?"

She told herself to tell him no. That she hadn't wanted company for years. Lots of years. And lots of months and weeks and days—she just couldn't remember precisely how many. But she knew she was lying. She did want company. She'd wanted company for years. Lots of years and months and weeks and days. She just hadn't allowed herself to have it. Not until one glorious night three weeks, six days, twenty hours and fifty-two minutes ago, a night she would carry with her forever. Even so, she couldn't bring herself to say that to Hogan.

"Anabel is friends with the Fleurys," he said. "She told me the view from their roof is spectacular."

"It is," Chloe replied.

He looked surprised. "So you've been up there?"

She nodded. She'd gone up to the Fleurys' terrace a number of times since coming to work for the

Fleurys. She didn't know why. The New York nights had turned cold and damp with winter setting in so solidly and hadn't been conducive to rooftop wanderings. But wander to the roof she had, over and over again. The view was indeed spectacular. She could see all of New York and Central Park, glittering like scattered diamonds on black velvet. But it had nothing on the view from Hogan's house. Probably because Hogan wasn't part of the view.

"Maybe you could show me?" he asked. "I mean, once you've finished with your party duties. Anabel said the Fleurys' parties tend to go pretty late, and she hates to be the first to leave."

"She was the first to leave at your party," Chloe said.

"That was because she was a woman on a mission that night."

"What mission?"

Hogan smiled again. But he didn't elaborate. "What time do you think you'll be finished?"

Chloe did some quick calculating in her head. "Maybe eleven?"

"Great. I'll meet you up on the roof at eleven."

She told herself to decline. Instead, she said, "Okay."

He looked at the tray. "What do you recommend?"

What a loaded question. All she said, though, was "Try the tapenade."

She remembered belatedly that he probably had

no idea what tapenade was and was about to identify the proper selection, but he reached for exactly the right thing. Her surprise must have shown on her face, because he told her, "I've been doing some homework."

And then he was moving away, fading into the crowd, and Chloe was able to remember she had a job she should be doing. A job that would fall just short of success because, like the hors d'oeuvres and so much more, nothing she did was quite right anymore.

Instead, the party went off without a hitch, and every dish was perfect—if she did say so herself. Even the moments when she served Hogan, where she feared she would spill something or misarrange something or forget something, all went swimmingly. By the time she finished cleaning up the kitchen—which also went surprisingly well—she was starting to feel like her old self again. Like her old cooking self anyway. The other self, the one that wasn't so focused on cooking, still felt a little shaky.

She had just enough time to go to her room for a quick shower to wash off the remnants of *Moules à la crème Normande* and *carottes quatre epices*. Then she changed into blue jeans and a heavy black sweater and headed for the roof.

Hogan was already there waiting for her. He'd donned a jacket to ward off the chill and stood with his hands in his pockets, gazing at the New York skyline in the distance. The full moon hung like a bright silver dollar over his head, and she could just make out a handful of stars higher in the night sky. Her heart hammered hard as she studied him, sending her blood zinging through her body fast enough to make her light-headed. Or maybe it was the simple presence of Hogan doing that. How had she gone nearly a month without seeing him? Without hearing him? Without talking to him and feeling the way he made her feel? How had she survived without him?

Although she wouldn't have thought he could hear her over the sounds of the city, he spun around the moment she started to approach. The night was cold, but the closer she drew to him, the warmer she felt. But she stopped when a good foot still separated them, because she just didn't trust herself to not touch him if she got too close.

"Hi," he said again.

"Hello."

"It's good to see you."

"It's good to see you, too."

A moment passed where the two of them only gazed at each other in silence. Then Hogan said, "So I looked up impracticability."

She barely remembered using that as an excuse to cancel her contract with him. How could she have wanted to do that? How could she have thought the only way to survive was to separate herself from

Hogan? She'd been dying a little inside every day since leaving him.

"Did you?" she asked.

"Yeah. I even used a legal dictionary, just to make sure I got the right definition. What it boiled down to is that one party of a contract can be relieved of their obligations if those obligations become too expensive, too difficult or too dangerous for them to perform."

"That about covers it, yes."

He nodded. "Okay. So I thought about it, and I figured it couldn't have become too expensive for you to perform your job, because I was paying for everything."

She said nothing in response to that, because, obviously, that wasn't the reason she'd had to leave.

"And it wasn't becoming too difficult for you to perform your job," he continued, "since you were excellent at it, and you made it look so easy and you seemed to love it."

"Thank you. And yes, I did love it. Do love it," she hastened to correct herself. Because she did still love to cook. She just didn't love cooking for the Fleurys as much as she'd loved cooking for Hogan. She hadn't loved cooking for anyone as much as she'd loved cooking for Hogan. Probably because it wasn't just cooking for Hogan she'd loved.

"So if you didn't think your job was too expensive or too difficult to perform," he said, "then you must have thought it was too dangerous."

Bingo. Because loving anything—or anyone—more than cooking was very dangerous indeed for Chloe. Loving anything—or anyone—more than cooking could very well be the end of her. At least that was what she'd thought since Samuel's death. Now she was beginning to think there were things much more harmful to her—and much more dangerous for her—than loving and wanting and needing. Like not loving. And not wanting. And not needing. She'd spent six years avoiding those things, and she'd told herself she was surviving, when, really, she'd been dying a little more inside every day. Losing more of herself every day. Until she'd become a shell of the woman she used to be. A woman who'd begun to emerge from that shell again the moment she met Hogan.

"Yes," she told him. But she didn't elaborate. She still didn't quite trust herself to say any of the things she wanted—needed—to say.

"So what was getting too dangerous?" he asked. "Were the knives too sharp? Because I can stock up on bandages, no problem."

At this, she almost smiled. But she still said nothing.

"Then maybe the stove was getting too hot?" he asked. "Because if that's the case, I can buy some fans for the kitchen. Maybe get a window unit for in there."

Chloe bit back another smile at the thought of a portable air conditioner jutting out of a window on the Upper East Side and dripping condensation onto the chicly dressed passersby below. She shook her head again. And still said nothing.

"Okay," he said. "I was hoping it wasn't this, but it's the only other thing I can think of. It was all that fresh, unprocessed whole food, wasn't it? I knew it. Someday scientists are going to tell us that stuff is poison and that boxed mac and cheese and tinned biscuits are the best things we can put in our bodies."

"Hogan, stop," she finally said. Because he was becoming more adorable with every word he spoke, and that was just going to make her fall in love with him all over again.

Then she realized that was ridiculous. She'd fallen in love with Hogan a million times since meeting him. What difference would one more time make?

"Well, if it wasn't the sharp knives, and it wasn't the hot stove, and it wasn't the allegedly healthy food, then what was it that made working for me so dangerous?"

He was going to make her say it. But maybe she needed to say it. Admitting the problem was the first step, right? Now if she could just figure out the other eleven steps in the How-to-Fall-Out-of-Love-with-Someone program, she'd be all set. Of course, falling *out* of love with Hogan wasn't really the problem, was it? Then again, she was beginning to realize that falling *in* love with him wasn't so bad, either.

"It was you, Hogan," she said softly. "It was the possibility of falling in love with you." Then she made herself tell the truth. She closed her eyes to make it easier. "No, that's not it. It wasn't the possibility of falling in love with you. It was falling in love with you."

When he didn't reply, she opened first one eye, then the other. His smile now was completely different from the others. There was nothing teasing, nothing modest, nothing sweet. There was just love. Lots and lots of love.

"You can't fight it, Chloe," he said. "Trust me—I know. I've been trying to fight it for a month. Trying to give you the room you need to figure things out. Trying to figure things out myself. But the only thing I figured out was that I love you."

Heat swamped her midsection at hearing him say it so matter-of-factly. "Do you?"

"Yep. And I know you love me, too."

"Yes."

For a moment they only gazed at each other in silence, as if they needed a minute to let that sink in. But Chloe didn't need any extra time to realize how she felt about Hogan. She'd recognized it the night they made love. She'd just been trying to pretend otherwise since then.

Hogan took a step toward her, close enough now for her to touch him. "Do you think you'll ever stop loving me?" he asked.

She knew the answer to that immediately. "No. I know I won't."

"And I'm not going to stop loving you."

He lifted a hand to her face, cupping her jaw lightly, running the pad of his thumb over her cheek. Chloe's insides turned to pudding at his touch, and she tilted her head into his caress.

"So here's the thing," he said softly. "If we both love each other, and neither of us is going to stop, then why aren't we together?"

She knew the answer to that question, too. Because it would be too painful to lose him. But that was a stupid answer, because it was going to be painful to lose him whether they were together or not. Okay, then because she would live in fear of losing him for the rest of her life. But that didn't make any sense, either, because if she wasn't with him, then she'd already lost him. Okay, then because... because... There had to be a reason. She used to have a reason. If she could only remember what the reason was.

"It's too late for us, Chloe," he said when she didn't reply. "We love each other, and that's not going to change. Yeah, it's scary," he added, putting voice to her thoughts. "But don't you think the idea of life without each other is even scarier?"

Yes. It was. Being alone since Samuel's death had been awful. Although she could deny it all she wanted, Chloe hadn't liked being alone. She'd tolerated it because she hadn't thought there was any other way for her to live. But she hadn't liked it. The time she'd spent living with Hogan and being with Hogan was the best time she'd had in years. Some years and some months and some weeks and some days she didn't have to keep a tally of anymore. Because she wasn't alone anymore. Or, at least, she didn't have to be. Not unless she chose to.

Hogan was right. It was scary to fall in love. No, it was terrifying. But the prospect of living the rest of her life without him was far, far worse.

"I want to come back to work for you," she said.

He shook his head. "Just come back. We'll figure out the rest of it as we go."

Chloe finally smiled. A real smile. The kind of smile she hadn't smiled in a long time. Because she was happy for the first time in a long time. Truly, genuinely happy. "Okay," she said. "But I'm still not going to cook you taco meatloaf."

Hogan smiled back. "No worries. We can share the cooking. I need to introduce you to the joys of chicken pot pie, too."

Instead of wincing this time, Chloe laughed. Then she stood up on tiptoe, looped her arms around Hogan's neck and kissed him. Immediately, he roped his arms around her waist and pulled her close, covering her mouth with his and tasting her deeply as if she were the most delectable dish he'd ever had.

Chloe wasn't sure how they made it to her bedroom on the first floor without alerting the dinner guests still lingering in the Fleurys' salon, since she and Hogan nearly fell down every flight of the back stairs on their way, too reluctant to break their embrace and shedding clothes as they went. Somehow, though, they—and even their discarded clothing—did make it. He shoved the door closed behind them, then pressed her back against it, crowding his big body into hers as he kissed her and kissed her and kissed her.

By now, she was down to her bra, and the fly of her jeans was open, and he was down to his T-shirt, his belt loosened, his hard shaft pressing against her belly. She wedged her hand between their bodies enough to unfasten the button at his waist and tug down the zipper, then she tucked her hand into his briefs to press her palm against the naked length of him. He surged harder at her touch, and a feral growl escaped him before he intensified their kiss. He dropped his hands to her hips, shoving her jeans and panties down to her knees, then he thrust his hand between her legs to finger the damp folds of flesh he encountered.

This time Chloe was the one to purr with pleasure, nipping his lip lightly before touching the tip of her tongue to the corner of his mouth. Hogan rubbed his long index finger against her again, then inserted it inside her, caressing her with the others until she felt as if she would melt away. With his free hand, he slipped first one bra strap, then the other, from her shoulders, urging the garment to her waist to bare her breasts. Then he covered one with his entire hand, thumbing the sensitive nipple to quick arousal.

Her breath was coming in quick gasps now, and her hand moved harder on his ripe shaft in response. He rocked his hips in time with her touches, until the two of them were *this close* to going off together. Just as the tightening circles of her orgasm threatened to spring free, he pulled their bodies away from the door and began a slow dance toward the bed. The moment they reached their destination, she yanked Hogan's shirt over his head, tossed it to the floor and pushed at his jeans to remove them, as well. Taking her cue, he went to work on removing what was left of her clothing, too.

When she turned to lower the bed's coverlet, he moved behind her, flattening his body against hers and covering her breasts with both hands. But when she bent forward to push away the sheets, he splayed his hand open at the middle of her back, gently bent her lower, and then, slow and deep, entered her from behind.

"Oh," she cried softly, curling her fingers tightly into the bedclothes. "Oh, Hogan…"

He moved both hands to her hips, gripping them tightly as he pushed himself deeper inside her. For long moments, he pumped her that way, the friction of his body inside hers turning Chloe into a hot, wanton thing. Finally, he withdrew, taking his time and caressing her fanny as he did, skimming his palms over her warm flesh before giving it a gentle squeeze. He tumbled them both into bed, lying on his back and pulling her atop him, straddling him. Instead of entering her again, though, he moved her body forward, until the hot feminine heart of her was poised for his taste.

His tongue flicking against her already sensitive flesh was her undoing. Barely a minute into his ministrations, Chloe felt the first wave of an orgasm wash over her. She moaned as it crested, waiting for the next swell. That one came and went, too, followed by another and another. But just when she thought she'd seen the last one, he turned her onto her back and positioned himself above her.

As he entered her again, another orgasm swept over her. But this time, Hogan went with her. He thrust inside her a dozen times, then emptied himself deep inside her. Only then did the two of them fall back to the bed, panting for breath and groping for coherent thought. Never had Chloe felt more satisfied than she did in that moment. Never had she felt so happy. So contented. So free of fear.

Loving wasn't scary, she realized then. Avoiding love—that was scary. Loving was easy. So love Hogan she would. For as long as she could. Because, *oh là là*, living without loving wasn't living at all.

It was a hot day in Brooklyn, the kind of summer day that cried out for something cold for dessert. So Chloe decided to add *tulipes de sorbet* to the daily menu of her new café, *La Fin des Haricots*. They would go nicely with the rest of the light French fare the little restaurant had become famous for in Williamsburg over the last year and a half, and it would make Hogan happy, since it was a reasonable compromise for the chocolate ice cream he preferred.

They'd compromised on a lot over the last eighteen months. He'd sold his grandfather's Lenox Hill town house, along with Philip Amherst's other properties—save the one in Paris, of course, where they planned to spend the month of August every year, starting with their honeymoon last summer. Then they purchased a funky brownstone they'd been renovating ever since, and in whose backyard Chloe had planted a small garden and built a small greenhouse. Hogan's chain of Dempsey's Garages was fast becoming reality—he was already operating three in the city and had acquired properties for a half dozen more. And *La Fin des Haricots* was fast becoming a neighborhood favorite. They worked hard every day and loved hard every night, and on Sundays…

Sundays were sacred, the one day they dedicated

completely to each other. Usually by spending much of it in bed, either eating or talking or loafing or—their favorite—making love.

Hogan's other passion in life was the scholarship fund he'd set up in his parents' names for kids from both his old and his new neighborhoods. He'd also donated significantly to Samuel's fund. The losses of their pasts would help bring happiness into others' futures, and that made the two of them about as rich as a couple of people could be.

Life was good, Chloe thought as she finished up the menu and handed it off to her head waiter to record it on the ever-changing chalkboard at the door. Then she buttoned up her chef's jacket—one that fit, since she had packed Samuel's away and wore her own now—and headed back to the kitchen. Her kitchen. She might still be cooking for other people, but it was in her own space. A space where she was putting down roots, in a place she would live for a very long time, with a man she would love forever. It still scared her a little when she thought about how much she loved her husband. But it scared her more to think about not loving him.

He met her at the end of her workday as he always did, on this occasion arriving at the kitchen door in his grease-stained coveralls, since it was the end of his workday, too. They ate dinner together at the chef's table, then, hand in hand, they walked home. Together they opened a bottle of wine. Together they enjoyed it on their roof. Together they made plans for their trip to Paris in August. And then together they went to bed, so they could make love together, and wake up together and start another day in the morning together.

Because together was what they were. And together was what they would always be. No matter where they went. No matter what they did. No matter what happened.

And that, Chloe thought as she did every night when they turned off the light, was what was truly *magnifique*.

\* \* \* \* \*

# COMING NEXT MONTH FROM

### Available May 9, 2017

## #2515 THE MARRIAGE CONTRACT
*Billionaires and Babies* • by Kat Cantrell
Longing for a child of his own, reclusive billionaire Des marries McKenna in name only so she can bear his child, but when complications force them to live as man and wife, the temptation is to make the marriage real...

## #2516 TRIPLETS FOR THE TEXAN
*Texas Cattleman's Club: Blackmail* • by Janice Maynard
Wealthy Texas doctor Troy "Hutch" Hutchinson is the one who got away. Now he's back and ready to make things right, but Simone is already expecting three little surprises of her own...

## #2517 LITTLE SECRET, RED HOT SCANDAL
*Las Vegas Nights* • by Cat Schield
Superstar Nate Tucker has no interest in the spoiled pop princess determined to ensnare him, but when a secret affair with her quiet sister, Mia, results in a baby on the way, he'll do whatever it takes to claim Mia as his.

## #2518 THE RANCHER'S CINDERELLA BRIDE
*Callahan's Clan* • by Sara Orwig
When Gabe agrees to a fake engagement with his best friend, Meg, he doesn't expect to fight temptation at every turn. But a makeover leads to the wildest kiss of his life and now he wants to find out if friends make the best lovers...

## #2519 THE MAGNATE'S MARRIAGE MERGER
*The McNeill Magnates* • by Joanne Rock
Matchmaker Lydia Whitney has been secretly exacting revenge on her wealthy ex-lover, but when he discovers her true identity, it's his turn to exact the sweetest revenge...by making her his convenient wife!

## #2520 TYCOON COWBOY'S BABY SURPRISE
*The Wild Caruthers Bachelors* • by Katherine Garbera
What happens in Vegas should stay there, but when Kinley Quinten shows up in Cole's Hill, Texas, to plan a wedding, the groom's very familiar brother's attempts to rekindle their fling is hindered by a little secret she kept years ago...

---

**YOU CAN FIND MORE INFORMATION ON UPCOMING HARLEQUIN® TITLES, FREE EXCERPTS AND MORE AT WWW.HARLEQUIN.COM.**

HDCNM0417

*Superstar Nate Tucker has no interest in the spoiled pop princess determined to ensnare him, but when a secret affair with her quiet sister, Mia, results in a baby on the way, he'll do whatever it takes to claim Mia as his.*

*Read on for a sneak peek at*
*LITTLE SECRET, RED HOT SCANDAL*
*by Cat Schield*

Mia had made her choice and it hadn't been him.

"How've you been?" He searched her face for some sign she'd suffered as he had, lingering over the circles under her eyes and the downward turn to her mouth. To his relief she didn't look happy, but that didn't stop her from putting on a show.

"Things have been great."

"Tell me the truth." He was asking after her welfare, but what he really wanted to know was if she'd missed him.

"I'm great. Really."

"I hope your sister gave you a little time off."

"Ivy was invited to a charity event in South Beach and we extended our stay a couple days to kick back and soak up some sun."

Ivy demanded all Mia's time and energy. That Nate had spent any alone time with Mia during Ivy's eight-week stint on his tour was nothing short of amazing.

They'd snuck around like teenage kids. The danger of getting caught promoted intimacy. And at first, Nate found the subterfuge amusing. It got old fast.

It had bothered Nate that Ivy treated Mia like an employee instead of a sister. She never seemed to appreciate how Mia's kind and thoughtful behavior went above and beyond the role of personal assistant.

"I don't like the way we left things between us," Nate declared, taking a step in her direction.

Mia took a matching step backward. "You asked for something I couldn't give you."

"I asked for you to come to Las Vegas with me."

"We'd barely known each other two months." It was the same excuse she'd given him three weeks ago and it rang as hollow now as it had then. "And I couldn't leave Ivy."

"She could've found another assistant." He'd said the same thing the morning after the tour ended. The night after Mia had stayed with him until the sun crested the horizon.

"I'm not just her assistant. I'm her sister," Mia said, now as then. "She needs me."

*I need you.*

He wouldn't repeat the words. It wouldn't do any good. She'd still choose obligation to her sister over being happy with him.

And he couldn't figure out why.

# Whatever You're Into... Passionate Reads

Looking for more passionate reads from Harlequin®?
Fear not! Harlequin® Presents, Harlequin® Desire and
Harlequin® Blaze offer you irresistible romance stories
featuring powerful heroes.

### ◆HARLEQUIN *Presents*

Do you want alpha males, decadent glamour and jet-set
lifestyles? Step into the sensational, sophisticated world of
Harlequin® Presents, where sinfully tempting heroes ignite a
fierce and wickedly irresistible passion!

### ◆HARLEQUIN *Desire*

Harlequin® Desire novels are powerful, passionate and
provocative contemporary romances set against a backdrop of
wealth, privilege and sweeping family saga. Alpha heroes with
a soft side meet strong-willed but vulnerable heroines amid a
dramatic world of divided loyalties, high-stakes conflict and
intense emotion.

### ◆HARLEQUIN *Blaze*

Harlequin® Blaze stories sizzle with strong heroines and
irresistible heroes playing the game of modern love and lust.
They're fun, sexy and always steamy.

Be sure to check out our full selection of books
within each series every month!

www.Harlequin.com

# Get 2 Free Books,
## Plus 2 Free Gifts—
### just for trying the Reader Service!

 HARLEQUIN *Desire*